The Reigns of Terror

Volumes One, Two, & Three

Jack Reigns

The Reigns of Terror and all stories within are works of fiction. Names, characters, places, and incidents either are the product of the author's imagination or are used fictitiously, except where explicitly noted. Any resemblance to actual persons, living or dead, events, or locales is entirely coincidental.

Cover design by Anna Chiara Stagi @stagah_artworks

Copyright © 2024 by Jack Reigns

Published by Jackalope Books LLC.
2810 N Church St.
PMB 991928,
Wilmington, Delaware 19802-4447

The scanning, uploading, recorded reading, and distribution of this book or any of the stories contained within, without written permission of the author, is theft of the author's intellectual property. If you would like permission to use material from this book (other than for review purposes) please contact Jackalope Books LLC. Thank you for your support of artist rights.

All rights reserved.

ISBN: 978-1-962427-03-6
ISBN: 978-1-962427-04-3 (eBook)

For Bean, and all the dreamers

Contents

Introduction 8

Labor Shortage 10

Hügelkultur 18

A Long Drive 25

The Superior Hunters 40

The Underground 55

A Good Prank 63

Potluck 81

The Cave 94

The Box 104

I Remember You 110

Burnout 121

The Bee Witch 132

It's A Girl 145

Thank You 157

Jack Reigns

Introduction

Sometimes a good horror short really hits the spot. A bite of terror before bed, or when you have a minute and need to escape from reality. It is perfect for when the mundane becomes overwhelmingly oppressive, or your own terrors are great enough you really need something fantastical to take your mind off them.

I harbor no illusions of being the next Hemingway. Many of my stories are entertaining, but not life changing. That's alright. The goal of the collection is to give you, the reader, a few minutes of respite from the horrors of life. I hope at minimum, you'll be amused, and on occasion, deeply unsettled.

The Reigns of Terror Volumes 1-3 pulls together all twelve short stories in the first three collections, plus a bonus story; Hügelkultur. It provides a more substantial meal than the snacks of Family, The Woods, and Ghosts each provide on their own. It is a meal meant to sustain for the duration of a novel, or is for those who prefer to read on paper instead of devices. If this is your first visit to The Reigns of Terror, welcome to my dark stories. I hope you have a horrific time.

May your dreams be forever haunted,

-JR

https://jackreigns.com/
https://www.instagram.com/jacksterbooks/
https://www.tiktok.com/@jacksterbooks
https://bsky.app/profile/jacksterbooks.bsky.social

Labor Shortage

Vikram stared out the window of the conference room, tuned out from the surrounding conversation.

"Vik?" His boss, Paul, had interrupted his thoughts. "What do you think?"

"Uh." Vikram couldn't remember what they'd been talking about. "Yeah, sounds good."

"There you go, folks." Paul threw his arms in the air. "We're going with the influencers."

Half the marketing team cheered while the other half grumbled in dissent. People around the table began gathering their things to head back to their desks. Those teleconferencing into the meeting said their goodbyes and disappeared from the large television at the front of the room. Vikram remained at the window, in a daze, eyes focused out the window.

"You okay, dude?" Paul asked.

"Huh?" Vikram tore his eyes away from the window, blinking as though he had forgotten where he was.

"You seem lost, out of it. You get enough sleep last night?"

"Oh, yeah, uh." Vikram rubbed his eyes. "Kids, right?"

"Toddlers!" Paul laughed. "Enough said. I miss it, but would never put myself through that again."

"Yeah, it's a lot sometimes."

Paul's laughter continued for a while as he walked out of the room. It echoed down the hall. Vikram rubbed his eyes again. The window pulled him back. He wasn't sure what it was out there that drew him so. The trees shimmered. It was hypnotizing. There didn't appear to be any wind other than at the spot he which drew him. He stood up. There was something about those trees, they were so beautiful.

Vikram headed towards the door.

"You going out for lunch, Vik?" Sadie, the front desk girl, was tapping her long nails on her desk while watching something on her phone.

"Yeah, just uh, just going for a walk." He pushed through the front door, ignoring her response.

The copse of trees was about a half mile away. To get there, you had to walk across the parking lot, through an intersection, scramble down and up an embankment, and cross a five-lane freeway, both directions. There you would find the patch of woods. Not even a park, just a heap of trees that no one had bothered to purchase and develop. Vikram had no recollection of having seen them before.. He walked with his eyes a smidge out of focus, hypnotized by what was in front of him. The leaves danced like waves of the ocean reflecting the sun.

Getting around the parking lot was easy. The intersection wasn't a problem. This was a large complex of office buildings and only saw heavy traffic at the beginning and end of the workday. He stumbled down the side of the ditch separating the freeway from the road that ran alongside it. Bushes tore at his jeans and the hem of his button-up plaid shirt. There were scotch broom and maple starts scenting the air, Vikram stumbled through them unaware. The first freeway lane he staggered into was an exit lane, and he made it through unscathed. A horn blared as an SUV went speeding by. The next two lanes were empty. In the last lane, a dad driving a sedan with three kids in the back stomped on the brakes to avoid slamming into him. It was promptly rear-ended by a pickup truck. All the airbags in both vehicles deployed. Vikram kept walking.

An SUV, a Range Rover, squealed as it also hit the brakes to prevent crashing into the thirty-something Indian man as he staggered across the freeway. It didn't stop in time. Driving the SUV was a woman who had recently been promoted to vice-president of her department, screamed as she braked. The massive vehicle managed to almost stop before hitting him. Vikram was knocked down on impact, sending him sprawling ahead of the vehicle, but he was not run over.

The woman jumped out of her car. "Oh my God! Oh my God!" she screamed and ran to check on him.

Vikram lay in a daze before crawling to his hands and knees.

"Are you okay?" the woman asked, helping him to stand.

Vikram nodded and continued walking towards the trees. It was the middle of the day, and no one was leaving the city yet. He made it across the opposite five lanes without issue.

~ ~ ~

The next day, Sadie approached Paul with a note. "Um, Paul?"

"Hmm?" He didn't bother to glance up from his laptop.

"Vikram's wife just called here again. She said she's going to call the police."

Paul looked up from his screen. "Alright, I don't know what else to tell her. I don't know why she thinks we'd know where he went last night."

"So, what should I tell her?"

"Tell her…" Paul blew out a loud sigh. "That, we'll call her if we hear from him, and that she should do whatever she needs to."

"Okay." Sadie slunk out of the room.

That afternoon, the logistics team ended their weekly check-in late. It had been Giorgio's birthday and there'd been treats, so the meeting ran long. They met in the conference room and opened all the blinds to let in the last of the early winter light. Most of the office was empty by the time they finished. The purchasing manager cornered the new intern on his way out. "Tanesa, can you clean up in here? Just leave the pizza in the breakroom fridge."

"Of course, no problem." She glanced around at the mess. Her girlfriend was going to be mad. She'd miss happy hour again.

"Good girl." The man stepped closer to her. "I wouldn't want anyone to think, you know, that we're dirty or anything." He raised one eyebrow and grinned when he said the word "dirty."

Tanesa flinched and wondered if that had been an effective tactic when he'd been sixty pounds lighter and twenty years younger. "I got it, it's fine." She ducked and twisted out around him.

He turned to watch her walk away. "Great." He called out. "Team player. That's what I like to see."

She gave him a thumbs up with one hand while surveying the extent of the mess left behind. The room emptied of people. Tanesa picked up the inadequate office waste bin and began shoving everyone's dirty refuse into it. At the far end of the table, the glint of the setting sun caught her eye. Out the window, the sky was a symphony of cotton candy pink fading into dusty violet and blue. The air shimmered where the last direct rays caught a subtle movement. A small grove of trees across the freeway caught her attention. They glowed, almost sparkling, a Christmas ornament in the firelight.

"What the?" she said aloud.

The sun set, and she realized she'd been standing there, staring at the trees for a while. She checked her phone. It was 7:26. "Shit."

She rushed through, shoving everyone else's paper plates, and napkins, and cups, and cutlery, into the bin until the trash towered above the sides. The bin was overflowing, and some items fell out. Tanesa groaned and walked outside to find the dumpster.

Once outdoors, the fresh air lifted her mood, and something called to her, pulling her to glance at the trees one more time. They were so stunning there, illuminated in the freeway streetlights. She gasped. Tanesa had never found nature so beautiful before. The branches danced in the breeze as they beckoned her to come join them in their soft, welcoming embrace. She dropped the waste bin and started across the parking lot.

~ ~ ~

Two weeks later, Paul rushed to grab the front desk phone before it stopped ringing. He picked it up just in time for the caller to hang up.

"Hey Paul?" Janet smirked as she walked past. "You our new front desk girl now?"

"Yeah, I decided my job wasn't challenging enough. Hey Janet?"

She stopped and tilted her head towards him, waiting.

"Where is everybody?"

"What do you mean?"

"Well." Paul set down the phone and ran his fingers through his hair, tugging on the ends. A bad habit that he was well aware he needed to stop. "Sadie didn't show up this morning. Half of marketing has quit without notice. That new supply chain intern bailed; she didn't even put the pizza away before she left. You're the first person to have showed up today, after me and Don. I have no idea what's going on. It's like somebody's pranking me right now."

"Maybe it was Rachel." Janet took a sip of her coffee and widened her eyes at him.

"Rachel?"

"Well yes, Paul. Our coworker killed herself by running into oncoming traffic. That's not something people just get over."

"Guess so, don't know. Figured it was something more, something else."

"I don't know Paul. I suppose nobody wants to work anymore." She shrugged and headed towards the breakroom.

Paul got up to make a loop through the office. He wanted to see if anyone had come in through the back door. The place was so empty the motion detector lights had turned off and blinked into startling brightness as he entered the open floor plan space. He grunted a small sound of annoyance and decided to find his boss, Don.

"Hey Don?" Paul entered the private office with a wave

and a knock on the wall. Once he'd interrupted a phone call with a major customer, the aftermath had made him sweat with fear of being fired for weeks.

Don stood with his back to the door, staring out of the large floor to ceiling windows which lined one wall of his office. The only rooms in the office with windows were this one, the breakroom, and the conference room.

"Don?" Paul asked again, coming up behind the older man.

"Oh, hey Paul. Sorry I didn't hear you enter. What can I help you with?"

Paul's cheeks grew red as he realized how ridiculous he was about to sound. He forged ahead anyhow. Sitting in an empty office was uncomfortable for him, gave him the heebie-jeebies.

"Don, you know where everybody is? Is there some kind of off-site going on?"

"No idea, Paul," Don continued to stare out the window. "Haven't heard anything. Say, have you ever seen those trees before?"

Paul came up alongside his boss and looked to where he was staring. It took a moment for him to find it, and once he did, he had no idea how he'd ever not spotted it before. "Well. Holy cow."

"I know!" Don clapped his hands. "Can you believe it?"

"Not at all. I wonder, how long has that been there for?"

"No idea. Feels recent but look at the size of those trees. No way those are transplants."

"No." Paul stepped closer to the window. "Definitely not."

"Hey." Don reached over and tapped Paul's hand without looking away from the view. "You wanna walk over there with me? Go check it out?"

"Yes." Paul nodded his head. "I think I do. I think I'd like that very much."

The two men left the building together, Don holding the door for Paul. They pointed out the trees as they walked, making sure they didn't lose sight of it.

"There it is!" Don pointed.

"Yup, yup, that's right. Right there." Paul caught Don's arm before he walked out in front of a car in the intersection. "Watch out there, Don. Don't need an accident before we get there."

"Oh! Right, right." Don glanced around, surprised to find himself standing at the crosswalk. He looked back up at the trees and continued studying them while waiting for the light to change. Paul tapped his shoulder and motioned. The light had changed, the walking signal was lit up.

The two men continued on, entranced with the trees ahead of them. They helped each other down and up the embankment separating the street from the freeway. Crossing the freeway was a fun game. They held each other back, searching for oncoming cars and urging each other to hurry when the way was clear. Helping in this way, they made it across both directions and reached the other side.

Here there was a small ditch filled with tall, wild grasses encircling the trees. The great branches and leaves shivered in anticipation. The men stopped, staring into the foliage with awe.

"Well, look at that, just look at it." Neither was sure which one of them spoke. The men held hands and entered the trees.

Hügelkultur

Rich stared at his wife, who, in turn, stared out the kitchen window without moving. They were discussing the strange man the neighbors had seen in their yard the night before. "I'm sure it was nothing. Just a guy from the neighborhood wandering through."

Kendall pointed out the window towards the three raised garden beds, their tops covered in smooth, fresh dirt. "I don't understand why you wanted to start gardening so much all the sudden. He was probably poking around in there. Looking for tools or something."

Rich placed his hand around her waist, pulling her closer to him. "We're composting, it's good for the environment. And we'll get fresh vegetables, think of the kids."

"Sure," she shrugged, "but we need to put a lock on the

gate or something. If it was that same guy I saw without pants on, I sure as hell don't want to see him again. Freak better stay away from our kids."

"Are you sure there's nothing you want to tell me?" Rich squeezed her side in an affectionate pinch.

"Uh, I don't have time for another man, not with two kids. You're all the emotional labor I can handle."

Rich scoffed, "Okay. Well, I'm going to go plant some seeds."

Kendall shrugged again and went to check on the children.

That night, Rich woke up, same time as always. He didn't need to check the clock to know it was twelve seventeen a.m. He laid there in the dark, blinking, until his bladder and thirst made him rise. Some nights he could go right back to sleep, others, it took a few hours.

After a quick trip to the bathroom, he found his way to the kitchen for a glass of water. The window over the sink showed the backyard illuminated in the moonlight. The raised beds were a disturbed mess.

"Fuck." He went to find his flip-flops.

Outside, the dirt among the beds was wrecked, dotted with hills and valleys. A bunch had been pushed off the top and lay on the grass below. He kneeled and began scooping it back into the bed with his cupped hands. The porch light flickered on, and he heard his wife call for him. He got up and half jogged to the open door where she stood looking out, face somewhere between asleep and confused. "Rats," he told her, "In the garden beds."

"Oh." was all she could manage, and returned to bed.

He cleaned up, changed into different pajamas, and joined her, now able to fall asleep.

The next day was Saturday, and he woke up late to the sounds of his boys playing loudly in their room down the hall. He groggily stumbled in to interrupt. "Hey guys, why don't you go play out in the backyard?"

The boys became grew quiet.

"What?" Rich asked.

"Mom's out there with her friend." One of them said.

"We don't like him," chorused the other.

"What? I'll go check it out." Rich scratched his head, stretched, and headed for the back door.

Outside, Kendall stood by herself, watering the rose bushes that bordered the yard. "Morning sleepyhead." She sang.

"Hey, uh, who are you out here with?" Rich asked.

"Um, nobody? Do you see anyone else out here?"

"The boys said you were out here with someone."

Kendall shut off the hose. "That's weird. It's just been me all morning. I drank my coffee on the lounger and then got up to water the roses."

"Huh." Rich scratched his head.

"Kids." Kendall smiled and pretended to lash him with the hose. "Coffee's still warm. You want some?"

Rich grimaced. "What happened to my beds?" He stormed across the yard to the raised beds, now thrashed again, dirt thrown everywhere. It was as if he'd never fixed them the previous night.

"It was like that when I got up. You didn't do that?"

"Kendall, what the heck? Why would I destroy my own garden?"

"I don't know. Why were you out here in the middle of the night? I don't know why you do anything. You used to be all about going to the gym and now you're gardening like there's no tomorrow. I can't keep up with your ADD brain."

Rich let out a loud groan of frustration and began piling the spilled dirt into the beds. Kendall shrugged and went inside. The rest of the day was icy between them, and they avoided further conversation.

Before bed, Rich rattled two sleeping pills out of the bottle he kept in his nightstand, and slept like the dead. The next morning, his boys shook him awake, excited. "Dad, someone destroyed your garden."

Rich jumped up and ran outside, only wearing his boxers and a threadbare shirt he liked to sleep in. The beds were again disturbed, with piles of dirt tossed everywhere. The branches and leaves which made up the mid-layer of the beds poked through in various places. The boys had followed him out to assess the damage. "Get back in the house!" he roared and ran for the shovel they kept on the side of the garage.

Several minutes later, he'd shoveled most of the contents back into the beds when Kendall came around, hands on her hips. "You can't scream at the kids like that. Especially not out here where everyone can hear you."

"Did you do this, Kendall? You hate them that much? You sneak out here and trash everything, trash my hard work? Is this some kind of 'fuck you' for all the late nights I've worked?"

"Oh, my fucking God, Rich." Kendall turned away. Over her shoulder, she tossed the words, "I didn't touch your shit."

He heard the door slam as he smoothed the last bit of dirt into place.

A little while later, the family was gathered, but apart, in the living room. He sat, drinking his coffee in silence, while around him Kendall read on her phone and the kids watched cartoons. The doorbell rang. Rich and Kendall's eyes met, and neither made a move to get up.

"I got it!" one of the boys yelled, followed by the other shouting, "no, me!" A racket of them wrestling towards the door echoed through the foyer. Rich jumped up and beat them to it.

On the porch was Esther, their elderly next-door neighbor. She stood wringing her hands and waiting with a somber look upon her face. "Hi Rich, do you mind if I come inside for a minute?"

"Sure, of course, come in." He held the door open wide. "Kendall hun, Esther's here."

"Oh!" Kendall rushed into the room. "Come in! Would you like some coffee, Esther?"

"No thank you. I only came by because I wanted to tell you something."

Rich leaned against the wall and folded his arms; suddenly aware he was still wearing his dirt covered boxers and shirt. "What's going on?"

"Well." Esther's voice shook in the way that some elderly women had. "I had to call the police last night, because I saw a naked man in my backyard."

"What?" Kendall and Rich spoke together, reminding him of the way they'd been back when they had first started dating. Then, they always in agreed with each other. Always understanding. It didn't work like that anymore.

Esther nodded and continued. "I got up last night for a drink of water, and there in the backyard, right next to your fence, was a young man. He was wearing a black t-shirt and no pants! Standing there next to my rhodies. I called the police, but by the time they came, he was gone."

"Oh Esther," Kendall patted the older woman on the shoulder, "I'm so, so sorry. How traumatizing."

"Pfft." Esther waved her hand in the air. I may have been married for over forty years, but I've seen a willy or two before then.

Rich snorted lightly and covered his mouth, pretending to scratch his cheek. "Well thank you for letting us know Esther, we'll certainly keep an eye out for this creep."

"Of course, that's why I wanted to tell you. Don't want someone like that getting near your boys."

"No." Kendall nodded. "Absolutely not. Ugh, how gross."

"I've got to get running," Esther walked towards the door. "It's Bingo Day down at the community center."

Rich saw her out and closed it firmly behind her, after thanking her again for stopping by. He walked into the kitchen where Kendall was sipping her coffee, staring into her phone. He knocked on the wall. "I think it's time you told me what's really going on."

Kendall looked up. "Going on?"

"Yes, what's going on, Ken? Who is this guy that keeps coming around?"

"I don't know Rich, maybe it's the same person who's fucking up your garden beds."

Rich huffed and walked away. He wanted to take a hot shower and think. Something wasn't right, and if Kendall wasn't going to confess, he had an idea of how to figure it out.

Rich didn't bother going to sleep that night. He waited. At fifteen minutes after midnight, he got up, pulled on his sneakers, and wandered outside to wait. It didn't take long.

The young man appeared next to the beds without having come from anywhere. He was young, still a teenager, and had messy brown hair that he wore a little chin length. His eyes were rimmed with heavy black eyeliner, which went with his black mesh t-shirt, torn at the places he'd been stabbed in his chest and abdomen. He was naked from the waist down and his limp penis resting on his ball sack gave the entire vision an almost comical element. The man waited silently and glared.

Rich sighed. "So, it was you."

The half-naked man took a step towards him, making no sound in the grass.

Rich cleared his throat and began again. "This has to stop."

The young man glared and threw his arms out over the raised beds.

Rich stepped forward. "I know, it sucks. I'd be mad too. But there wasn't any other option."

The man opened his mouth and shaped silent words. Tears leaked from his eyes without a sound. He motioned to the beds and back to Rich.

"Okay, okay, I'll tell your mom something. That you ran away or something, so she stops looking for you."

The dead man closed his eyes and continued crying. The moonlight grew brighter and filtered through his body, making him almost transparent.

"You didn't leave me any choice. You said if I didn't tell her, you would. I loved you, alright, but I can't just give up my family for some fucking femboy. You made me do it. You pushed me too far."

The ghost was shaking now, violently ugly-crying, and crumpled to the ground.

Rich pointed at the ghost. "Stop fucking with my gardens. Stop fucking with my family and stop fucking with the neighbors. If you do this again, I'll dig up all your pieces and dump them on your mother's front porch. Got it?" He didn't wait for an answer before stomping back towards the house.

The ghost let himself melt into the ground.

Days, then weeks, went by without disturbance and the beds remained untouched. Rich took pills every night to sleep. He was up to 5 at a time. Some nights, the pills alone wouldn't cut it and he had to throw in a few beers, and eventually a case or bottle of wine. The garden grew amazing produce that year.

A Long Drive

Chuck and Brian finished their day and threw their gear into the bed of Chuck's truck, a 1989 Chevy C10. The two men worked as tree-fallers, also known as loggers, and had started for the show before dawn. They were ready to go and find a hot meal. The men were hours from home, nestled into a cranny somewhere between the smaller mountains surrounding the great overseeing Mount Adams. High above them loomed the giant mountain at unexpected turns, poking out above the dirt and gravel roads in Gifford Pinchot National Forest. On the dash, the clock announced it was just after five in the evening.

At first, they filled the cabin with exhausted silence. Then, after a bit, they drove in awkward silence. Chuck was lost in his thoughts, decompressing as he did on the way home. Brian was new to the team. He'd said that he'd logged before on another outfit, but Chuck had noticed he'd made a lot of mistakes today. Everyone had noticed. After the third slipup, they'd moved him over to chokersetting for the rest of the day. Someone needing to be taught the ropes did not normally bother him, but out here ego and mistakes could hurt someone. Hell, they could kill you. This wasn't the type of situation in which you wanted to lie to get ahead.

"Nice rig." Brian offered, "'88?"

"89," Chuck corrected him, throwing an eyebrow up. "Good eye."

"It handle OK?" Brian ran his hands over the dash. The truck was organized and clean inside, although a little dusty from cigarettes and daily commutes through the woods.

"I like it." Chuck tapped the steering wheel. "I'm a Chevy man. They hold up. Gotta buy American."

"You ever think about selling it?"

"This? Nah, she's only 6 years old."

An awkward lull filled the cab. Chuck's voice was coarse from the dust they'd been inhaling all day. "If you're in the market, I know a guy down in Astoria. They might have some used trucks on the lot."

"Yeah, thanks, that'd be great." Brian's voice was too loud. He realized as soon as he uttered the words.

Chuck nodded and adjusted his hat, a snapback with the Mondale for America logo across the front. The white letters were tinged beige from wear.

He had only picked up Brian as a favor to the foreman. They lived a couple miles away from each other, which was as about as close to next door as loggers ever got. Riding up together saved time and ensured more men made it to the show on schedule. They had a lot of land to clear and things could go off the rails quick. A sizable chunk of time could be lost for stupid reasons. Any place where they could save time would be worth it. Everyone knew that. Except, it seemed, for Brian.

Brian had the right appearance of a timberfaller; heavy beard, close cut hair, worn work clothes that smelled of sweat and labor. But that was also the style these days. Kids who didn't even know how to change a tire on their daddy's sedan were growing beards and wearing plaid flannel. Brats who'd never worked outside of a desk or fast-food counter were buying work boots and sweatshirts with reflectors on them. Chuck didn't understand it. Whatever, all Brian needed to do was carry his own weight and not get anyone injured or killed. Welp, they'd see.

It seemed as though it was getting dark earlier. Chuck exhaled through his nostrils and switched on his head lights. Oh crap, it was August. It *was* getting dark earlier. It was important to be sure anything in the road wasn't something that would mess things up further, a wild animal, a fallen rock, a hole. A blown tire might leave you out here overnight. They'd left a bit late for the day and now Chuck had to worry until they found pavement.

The new guy cleared his throat. "Guess I kinda mucked up first day out."

Chuck eyed him and then gave a curt nod. "Some days it's like that. Tomorrow will be better."

Brian nodded, matching Chuck. "First day nerves, all that bullshit." Then let out a braying laugh, which enveloped the cab of the pickup.

Chuck remained stoic, "yup."

"You said you've been a lumberjack for 15 years?"

Chuck eyed him. "Been falling for 14. Where'd you say you

were from again?"

Brian flew into a coughing fit. His face turned red, and he beat on his chest. Chuck reached over and gave a hard whack on his back. The younger man caught his breath, and they fell back into stillness. Time droned on.

Out here, radio stations were spotty, not worth trying for. The truck took cassettes, but they didn't have any. Chuck was used to sorting his thoughts after a long day, surrounded by the noise of chainsaws. Now, with company, it felt uncomfortable, as if he wasn't doing something important that needed to be done. He thought about who else might live close to this guy.

Brian cleared his throat again. Apparently, he was the kind of person who couldn't handle sitting quiet for too long. In his head, Chuck crossed out the possibility of a fishing buddy.

Brian finished clearing his throat. "Seems like this road has gone on for a long time. Longer than I remembered."

Chuck thought and surveyed the packed dirt and gravel road in front of them. "Seems that way. Huh." He'd been thinking about the new guy, not paying attention. Now he wondered if he'd missed his turn. "I guess it's just because it's been a long day."

"You, uh, you think Park's going to be alright?"

Chuck nodded. "You gave him quite a scare, but just a scare." He flared his nostrils. "He'll live. It'd be for the best if you pay more attention to the side you're falling on though."

"Yeah," Brian's voice eeked out, and his cheeks grew red. "It's uh, it's been a while since I done this kind of work. Guess I got rusty."

"Hmm." Chuck's head swiveled towards him and, at the last moment, turned back to the road. "Where'd you say you moved from again?"

"Oh, uh, Montana."

"Montana." Chuck's voice was flat, dry. "What'd you clear out there?"

"Uh, pine, fir, spruce."

"Spruce?"

"Yeah, well, sometimes."

Chuck tried to recall if he remembered any of the landmarks they passed. He thought there should be a medium-sized boulder right before the turn. They'd been on this road for a while, much longer than usual. "You said the wife brought you out to Naselle?"

"Uh, yeah, kinda."

"What's the Mrs. name?"

"Ky…" Brian's voice faded out before coming back in strong, "Ra. Kira."

"Kira?"

"Yup."

Chuck nodded, bobbled, and then nodded again. "My wife packed a roast beef sandwich for my lunch today. Every time she packs a sandwich, I've got to check it. A while back, she kept complaining that I ate so fast I never stopped to appreciate the work she put in and then one day I came home, and she asked if I'd enjoyed my sandwich. She was all smug, arms folded. Shoulda known something funny was going on. I told her I noticed it was a little dry and the woman about fell over laughing. I guess she'd wrote me a note on a piece of paper and tucked it inside the sandwich, figured I'd take a bite, find it and laugh. I'd ate the whole damn thing."

Both men laughed. Brian tapped the dashboard a few times. "They just have no idea how hungry hard work makes you."

"No idea at all." Chuck shook his head and laughed again.

"Truth is, if she sent me with a can of dog food, I'd be so hungry at lunch I'd eat it. Can't tell her that, though."

"Absolutely not!" Brian sat straight up. "Once Ky…ra burnt the meatloaf so bad it crunched. Still ate it."

Chuck smiled. "You better. You'll be in for a world of hurt if you don't."

"Don't I know it."

Chuck pulled the truck over. "Hey, I'm not sure how, but I think I missed the turn somewhere. We should have hit it a while back, at least fifteen minutes ago. We need to go back, shouldn't take too long."

Brian shrugged, "makes sense."

They dropped conversation as Chuck worked the truck through a five point turn on the narrow forest road. On this section, one side dropped fast to a steep boulder field. Going over the edge there might result in the truck getting stuck at best, tumbling down the hill at worst. The ambient light had nearly faded out from the day.

The other side of the road angled upward into a steep face that the road had been carved out of. There was about a foot or two of brush before hitting the wall of granite. Going off the road here they'd be more likely to get a tire stuck in the drainage ditch that ran alongside. A storm here was a real danger if the road didn't have drainage on both sides. Sometimes these mountain storms were brief, but furious, more than any regular vehicle was built to drive in.

"What's that?" Brian's voice rose a few pitches, leaning forward towards the windshield.

"What's what?" Chuck asked, watching the road as he executed the maneuver.

"Out there in the rocks, I just saw something white and huge."

Chuck shook his head, "dead tree maybe. They sometimes

shine white in the headlights."

"Not a tree. It was moving. It was coming at us."

"Dear probably. Maybe Elk. Could have been a sheep. A couple of guys have said they've seen a mountain goat out here before, but I've never."

"Mountain goat." Brian let out a slow whistle.

"You seen one before?"

"Not like that."

"Huh," Chuck straightened out the truck, then rolled down the window a bit and lit a cigarette with the truck's lighter before resuming speed.

Brian opened his mouth to ask a question when the truck hit something large and bucked upwards. Both men were tossed in their seats and Chuck slammed on the brakes.

"What was that?" Brian rubbed his temple where it had knocked against the door frame.

Chuck jerked back and forth, looking outside for anything to explain what they just hit. He put the truck into park and jumped out the door, sending up a small dust cloud with his landing. Behind the truck, the road lay flat, no noticeable debris. Underneath was also clear. He opened the driver's side door. "There's nothin. You see a critter?"

Brian shook his head no.

"There's no blood anyhow. Something must have run under the truck, must not have been hurt too bad to make it back to the trees."

Brian shrugged and looked around for any sign of an injured animal.

Chuck kicked the driver's side rear tire twice and climbed back in. He started the truck in silence and eased it forward a few feet. There was no sign of problems or damage. They continued down the road.

Brian broke first. "Well, that sure was weird."

"Eh," Chuck snorted. "Weird things happen out here."

"Weird how?"

"Oh, ya know, people see things. Daryll, back at the show, says he saw Bigfoot once."

"Bullshit."

"Yup, says he saw it while falling up in Okanogan County."

"Wouldn't that be something? You don't believe him, do you?"

Chuck glanced at his passenger out of the corner of his eye. "What do you think?"

A moment of tension floated between them, before both men burst out laughing. They were still laughing when, up ahead, a large dark shape moved across the road. Chuck slowed to a stop.

Brian's voice came out higher pitched this time. "What was that?"

Chuck sat, quiet, staring straight ahead. He gripped the wheel tight, knuckles white. He cleared his throat and spoke. "I...I didn't get a good look at it. Bear, maybe. What'd you see?" He snatched a quick, full glance at Brian, who was sitting straight up and pushed back in his seat.

"What did I see?"

The two men looked at each other, waiting for the other to elaborate.

"What I saw," Brian began, "was a great big black shadow just slide across the road. I didn't see no bear, Chuck."

Chuck clenched and unclenched his jaw, chewing an invisible wad of tobacco. "Well, something had to cast that shadow, didn't it?"

Brian stared back, wide-eyed, taking occasional quick glances to the path ahead of them..

The older man continued, "Something cast that shadow, so

something walked by, but all we saw was the shadow. That's all. That's all it was."

Brian's eyes darted around between the road ahead and at his coworker next to him. "You bring me out here to mess with me, Chuck? Some kind of new guy hazing ritual?"

Chuck's face clouded. "I don't play those kinds of games. Seen enough good men get hurt out here to waste time playing grab-ass and snipe hunt."

"Okay," Brian took a deep breath, "I didn't mean nothing. That was, that thing. I've never seen something have a shadow like that before."

Chuck took his foot off the brake and began moving forward again. "A lot of weird things out in the woods, friend. Can't let 'em spook you or you'll never last."

The two rode on, one man thankful for the quiet and one man searching for words. Brian rolled down his window, pulled out a cigarette and lighter, lit it, and took a deep, long drag. "You ever get tired of this drive?"

Chuck rolled his head from side to side, stretching his neck, and shrugged. "I don't mind. I think the wife minds me being gone for so long. Gotta make a living though."

Brian forced a short laugh. "Yeah."

The two slipped into silence again. After twenty minutes, Chuck began shifting in his seat, slowing down and looking out the side windows. Brian fidgeted and thought about lighting another cigarette.

"What's going on Chuck?"

"The turn. We should have passed it by now. But I don't see it anywhere." He slowed to a stop, put the truck in park, and climbed down out of the vehicle. Brian followed him out and stretched his arms. They'd been driving for well over an hour now. It should have been only twenty or thirty minutes from the site to the turn down the mountain.

A noise whistled through the air, as loud as if a bird had sung right in their ears. Both men jerked upright and spun, searching for the cause. Brian kicked at the gravel and stomped his feet, shaking off an invisible coat. "The hell was that?"

He looked up at Chuck to see the other man already climbing back into the truck in a hurry. Brian ran around to the passenger door and climbed in beside him, slamming the door lock down as soon as the latch clicked.

The two men looked to one another, unsure. Something large slammed into the back of the truck, rattling the vehicle forward several inches. Both of them screamed out in terror. Chuck jammed the keys into the ignition and the truck roared to life. They took off flying up the road.

After a couple minutes, a turnoff became visible ahead. A right turn, the way the turn to the site would be. Brian hit Chuck on the shoulder and pointed. The truck slid in the gravel as Chuck braked hard and dust flew as they turned right. They crashed into a giant cedar tree.

Chuck and Brian were thrown forward. Chuck was wearing his seatbelt and smashed his forehead into the steering wheel. Brian had smacked his face onto the dash, and now sat upright, holding his bleeding nose in his hands. There was no turn, it was only a brief widening in the road. A dead end into the forest. They sat stunned.

"Fuck." Brian muttered, pulling his shirt up over his face to contain the flow of blood.

Chuck shuddered, dazed. He shifted into reverse and backed it out, turning around so that they were facing the direction they had come. Shadows were getting longer. The air had become cool. He popped open the door and climbed down with the tentative movements of a man twice his age. The front grill had a pretty big dent in the middle. One headlight had cracked. They hadn't been going fast enough to cause any actual damage. Chuck climbed back in and pushed the lock down into place after shutting the door. Without a word, he started the truck up and went back the way they had come.

The men rode in silence again. Soon the shadows were long enough that the headlights were clearing bright paths into the road ahead.

"Fuck." Brian groaned again and let the shirt fall from his face. Blood coming out both nostrils was drying into crusty lines. In trying to stem it, he'd smeared it across his cheeks and chin, into his beard and down his neck.

"Sorry," Chuck said. "I thought it was the way to the show."

"Me too." Brian sounded stuffy and had to breathe through his mouth. "Hey, over there!"

Chuck looked up to where Brian was pointing. Another turn in the road, this one familiar. The truck slowed down to a near stop before swinging into the turn. A gravel road illuminated, unmistakable in the headlights. Chuck laughed and tapped the dash. Brian huffed a sigh a relief. They turned down the road.

It should have been only a few minutes before the road began winding down the mountain, before they found pavement. Instead, they continued on a straight line, the path rising and falling in small degrees. Brian had closed his eyes, relieved by the thought that in another hour, they'd be back in civilization. He felt the truck slow and begin backing up. "Hey." his eyes snapped open. "What are you doing?"

"This isn't our road." Chuck told him, while watching over his shoulder in order to back the truck up, making sure not to veer into the brush.

"Wait, a second." Brian sat up and turned to his coworker.

"This is the first turn, the first turn we've seen tonight. It has to be our road."

"I've driven this route every day for the past three months. This ain't our road." Chuck had found a place wide enough to turn around in and backed up into it. He shifted into drive. They began back the way they'd come at a crawl.

"How the hell, can it not be our road?"

"Watch your language when you're speaking to me." Chuck brought the truck to a stop. The two men eyed one another. "If you don't like the way I'm driving, you're welcome to hop on out and walk."

"Wait just a second now," Brian shrunk back into himself, "I didn't mean it that way. I just meant, how can that be? How is it possible?"

"Don't know." Chuck looked ahead and began accelerating. "But it's not our road home. Must have found an old logging road or something. Maybe some brush covering it got blown away or drug off by an animal."

"Drug off by an animal." Brian's shoulders dropped. "For that matter, where the heck are all the other guys, huh? We weren't the last ones to leave. We should have seen some of them by now, right?"

"Don't know," Chuck stared straight ahead. All the blood was gone from his hands.

"Don't you at least have a map or something?"

"Map!" Chuck tapped his temple and motioned at the dash. "Check the glove compartment."

Brian opened the cubby and found a folded-up map of Gifford Pinchot National Forest Routes and Motorways. Chuck slowed to a stop as they spread the map out across the dashboard. They traced the US Forest Service roads with their fingers, trying to find their location, when something crashed into the tailgate, knocking them both forward. Brian hit his forehead on the dash again, this time missing his nose. He yelled out in pain and frustration while slapping at the door to find the already pushed-down lock. he turned to see Chuck doing the same. Their eyes met.

Chuck shoved the map off the dash, crumpling it onto Brian and took off driving. They flew down the road for several minutes before Chuck let the truck slow to a crawl again. The vehicle crept forward by the pull of the engine.

"What's the matter?"

Chucked looked over at Brian's face. His forehead getting hit had caused his nose to leak blood again, but this time only a trickle. There was enough ambient light left outside to make out the bright red against the darker color of the younger man's beard. It was the same color red as the flannel shirt he wore. "We should have made it back to the other road by now."

Brian looked around, wild-eyed. He toggled between the view outside the windows and back to the driver, repeating the sequence several times before settling on Chuck's face. "How do you know?"

"I checked the odometer when we turned." Chuck tapped on the wheel as he spoke. "I made a note of the number and counted down after I turned around. We should have hit the other road a half mile back."

"You've got to be wrong."

Chuck's eyebrows crunched, heavy over his face. His lip curled, about to set Brian straight.

Brian put his hands up, a gesture of surrender. "Let's just go a little further."

The two rested in a stalemate. Chuck glared, eyes burning from the force of it. "Alright," he said, "alright." They sped up.

Another mile turned over on the odometer, and then

another after that. Both men watched the numbers change without saying a word. A loud bang and a lurch. Brian yelled out in terror.

The truck began limping with a jerky gait. The driver's side rear tire had blown. Chuck brought it to a stop, and they waited, staring out the front windshield, watching the gravel road in the brightness of the headlights. He reached over and pulled a small flashlight out of the glove compartment.

"Chuck," Brian put his hand on the other man's shoulder. "Wait."

"We can't drive on a flat, Brian. Whatever is going on here, we need to be able to get out of it. We can't do that with a flat. Now I got a spare in the back. I can change it in five minutes even. Here." Chuck reached under his seat and felt around for a second before pulling out a small .22 caliber semi-automatic pistol. "I want you to keep an eye on me, alright? Can you do that? Make sure there're no bears or cougars that come to cart me away while I'm changing the tire?"

Brian nodded. "Bears or cougars," he said, "yeah."

Chuck pushed the small pistol into the man's hands and squeezed Brian's shoulder back. The two gave each other a last nod. Chuck reached up and turned on the cab light, then lifted the lock on his door.

The door swung open with ease to an empty portion of the road. The bright cab light spilled, bright enough to turn anything beyond the circle into a black darker than the night. Chuck swung his legs out and landed with a solid thump onto the ground. He stood there, shining the beam of the small flashlight around him. He took several meager steps forward and turned the beam to the damaged tire to inspect it.

Brian sat, watching with wide eyes, pistol pointed out in front of him, barrel angled down so he wouldn't spook and shoot Chuck. The older man stepped out of the ring of light cast from the cab and bent down to better inspect the tire. Some scuffling noises came, then stopped.

Seconds passed. A scream and a thumping, dragging sound erupted into the night, which deteriorated back into nothing.

"Chuck?" he yelled, "Chuck?"

More quiet. His breathing came shallow and too fast. A moment of hesitation before he dove forward, grabbed the truck door, and slammed it shut in one quick motion. His hand shook as he slapped for the pin lock, shoving it down into place.

"Chuck?"

The truck shook in response. Brian screamed.

The Superior Hunters

The four women sat in their hunting blind, drinking wine from little paper boxes that they'd found at Jack's Country Store. It was long past when they expected any grazing game to come through. Now they were just relaxing and enjoying the warm fall day.

Becca's husband, Jorge, owned the blind, and his boss owned the land. A week ago, the wives (well, three wives and a forever fiancé) had gotten into a drunken argument with their partners about who could hunt better.

"We're all better shots," Alma yelled before tripping over nothing and stumbling backwards into her seat on the couch.

"Maybe at the range," Finn, Abbie's husband, had jeered, thrusting his tallboy at them. "But I bet you girls couldn't hit shit in the woods if it were thrown in your faces." Abbie made herself smaller beside him on the loveseat and took a sip of her beer.

Gina, engaged to Darren for the last 9 years, sputtered, "well maybe if you rednecks took us hunting the way Jorge takes Becca, we'd have proven how much bett..hic..better, we are."

Darren raised one eyebrow in that way he had that completely distorted his face into something demented. "You gonna clean an elk, Gin? You gonna pull out its guts and scrape the hide?"

Becca was the only one not completely wasted at that point. She was quiet, and usually underestimated. "I've done it. Jorge showed me how, I even did one by myself. I can show you how, Gina."

"I'm in!" Alma had jumped back to standing, beer raised high in the air. "I used to help my gramma clean chickens and I always clean my own trout!"

"Don't you Mexicans ever just buy meat at the grocery store like normal people?" Alma's husband, Gauge, laughed at his joke and reached up to pinch her butt.

She swatted his hand away. "Maybe I clean you and I don't need to go to the grocery store for a year fatass."

"Woah!" The others exclaimed.

Jorge threw an empty can at Gauge's head. It bounced harmlessly off his shoulder.

"Hey!" yelled Gauge.

"Hey!" Jorge shot back. "I told you to knock that shit off."

Gauge shrugged and gave a meek smile, as though helpless against the jerk comments that flowed from his unconscious towards his mouth while bypassing most of his brain. He and Alma had been married the longest. They also fought the meanest.

The next day, the women had flooded their group text with

indignation. A plan was made. The men were more than happy to support, being so sure they would be proven the better hunters. Not to mention, an impromptu boys' weekend was never a bad thing. Only Abbie and Becca had kids yet. Arrangements with grandparents covered any babysitting needs. Both Abbie's mom and Becca's stepmom told them, "No mercy."

Various girlfriends outside the immediate group offered to help. One well-meaning, but not very bright friend, had offered to help them cheat with venison from her own freezer. She was politely declined.

Fortified with the knowledge that a whole network of friends and family were now placing bets on the situation, the women became even more determined and planned relentlessly. Private land meant no permits needed. The group met at the range twice in the next week as a team, siting each other in at 50, 100, and 200 yards until they could take an eye out of a grouse at twilight.

The next Friday night, they took off for camp.

It was a two-and-a-half-hour drive into the woods on old logging roads, no longer serviced, unless Jorge's boss had gravel hauled up. That was the main reason he shared his land, to get donations towards keeping the roads in working order. Although in this circumstance, he had happily let the ladies enter for free. "Go get em," he'd told the two pickups as they passed through the gate he'd unlocked. He had daughters. They were excited to hear the ending of this story.

The land bordered thousands of acres of reservation land and national forest. At places there was no cell service, and it was often spotty where you could pick it up. Jorge had loaned them his satellite phone and GPS beacon. While inwardly sure they were going to come back somewhere between empty handed and with a good amount of meat, he kept his thoughts to himself and helped Becca load up with every piece of gear he'd shown her how to use.

The women had driven to a small mountain peak where a flat area with good visibility had been carved out and the view stretched for miles during the day. After dark, it was an ocean of pure black where the stars shone brighter than you could believe was possible. The women all rolled into one large tent for the night, having gone to bed sober, ready to wake before dawn and begin the stakeout.

Early Saturday morning they'd risen, roused by the alarm on a phone. They made instant coffee and packed snacks, a picnic lunch with cartons of wine, cold brews in cans, and set out for the blind. Setting up by five in the morning had allowed them to watch the glow of the valley light up like an orchestra tuning the day. The woman had sprayed themselves down with stink right after leaving the truck and laughed, making jokes that it was no worse than any of their husband's socks left in the laundry basket for a week.

The location was perfect, should have been perfect. A natural valley filled with lush grasses and small berry bushes typically attracted herds all season, and often the predators who followed them. The blind was on the ground, up on top of a slope, which allowed them a wide view across the valley with little blocking the way. If the day had gone right, they'd be cleaning and packing up more meat than they could carry by now.

Yet nothing arrived that morning. The women had taken turns dozing, snacking, and talking quietly, careful to keep their voices to no more than an occasional murmur. By ten, they had all but given up and started in on the wine. Loosely planning friendsgiving had been the topic at hand when Alma hushed them.

She was pinned to her scope, staring down something in

the valley and motioned with one hand for the others to look. The women lined up their rifles, two .308s. One 30.06, and Alma, with Gauge's AR-15. The other woman had looked at her with disbelief when she unloaded it from the case. "It's all Gauge would let me take," she said. "Besides, he told me they were sold as hunting rifles once."

"I guess if we get attacked by a bear, Alma has us covered." Abbie gave her a wink.

"That's right, I'm Rambo, I got your backs!" Alma knew that while she might struggle to hit a target, this would even the odds of hitting anything. The men were probably laughing right now about how the women could take a semi-auto hunting and still come back empty-handed.

Now the women sat still at their scopes, waiting for what Alma had sited to come into view. One by one, they saw it. Across the valley, slightly hidden by the trees at the border. A massive set of antlers moving carefully between trees. They watched them dip and rise; larger than any pair they'd seen before. A group in awe, silence pervaded until at last Becca slid in a soft question. "Who's going to take it?"

"I want it." Abbie was the quiet one, and now when she spoke, the group murmured their support. She didn't take the lead often at anything. The other women waited patiently, watching the horns catch the dappled sunlight through the remaining fall leaves. Abbie had the 30.06, even if she didn't kill it immediately as long as she hit, the animal wouldn't make it far.

They made themselves as still as possible. Abbie's slow, controlled breath became the only noise as she lined her site up with the rise and fall of her chest. The crack of the shot rang out. The antlers thrust high up into branches and a thunderous growl echoed across the valley. A deep guttural noise of a grizzly's roar sounded layered under a mountain lion's scream. The branches across the valley parted.

A head like an elk, but three times the size came through the leaves and stared across to where the women sat, watching. Following the head came the largest set of antlers any of the women had seen or heard of. Dozens of points on each side brought the antlers to a peak several feet above the top of the creature. Its nostrils flared, and it snorted, locked on to their location. It stepped into the clearing.

The head lifted as it moved forward until an animal over twenty feet tall entered the field, standing on its hind legs. The neck widened into a broad, bear like chest which spread into massive, clawed paws. The paws flexed as though a cat were kneading its bed, like it was thinking something over. The large, barreled chest narrowed into thinner thighs that further slimmed into hoofed legs. A large bloody mess covered one of the beast's thighs. It groaned and started towards them.

Becca made a choking noise and froze while the other three women scrambled backwards. Alma scrambled out of the blind, diving for cover underneath a large bush nearby. Abbie leaned forward and aimed her rifle at the monster a second time. Lining up the shot faster this time, she fired and watched, and the beast's shoulder rocked backwards. It halted, then leaned over and licked its blood, looked back to the women, and began running towards them.

"Hide!" Gina screamed, running out of the blind and dropping her rifle. She found a maple tree and scurried up the trunk to hide in the branches.

Becca grabbed Abbie's arm, "Run, Abbie. Run!" The two hustled away and began running as fast as they could, back towards the truck. A roar echoed across the forest, sounding like the one before, but angrier. They were still running when they heard the scream. They tripped, stumbled, caught each other, and kept running.

Back at the blind, the monster ripped the structure from the ground and threw it into the tree Gina had climbed. She nearly fell from her branch, caught herself and dangled for a brief moment before pulling herself back onto the thin branch. The beast strode towards her.

Its black eyes were on the same level as hers as it regarded her clinging to the branch. The beast began to move its head towards her, catching its antlers on the branches of the tree. It pulled back, looked around, angled its head and moved in again. Gina screamed a second time as it opened its wide jaws, showing a mix of omnivore teeth, including large fangs where the canines grew. It wrapped its jaws around her head as she sat frozen in fear. It crunched down.

From the ground, Alma watched in fear as it pulled Gina down from the tree by her face and shook her lifeless body voraciously until the body snapped away from the neck and fell to the ground. Alma's entire body felt numb as she retreated into her mind.

The beast dropped the head and walked over to where the blind had sat. A mess of camping chairs, water bottles, empty wine boxes and a knocked over cooler were strewn among loose ammunition, gear, and Gina's .308. It picked up her gun and held it between both paws, inspecting the device. Placing a mitt on either end of the barrel, it twisted and forced the barrel into a wide curve, then tossed the useless weapon aside. The creature huffed and nodded, then stomped off the way that Becca and Abbie had run.

Alma sat in the brush for a while before finding the bravery needed to creep out. She was shaking violently and freezing cold despite the seventy-two-degree day. She stood over the headless body of her friend and threw up, turning at the last second to not let the vomit land on Gina. She realized as she puked, she was still holding the AR tightly in her hands.

After spitting out the last of the vomit, she found her water bottle amidst the mess and swished her mouth clean. She turned the safety off her gun and started after her friends.

It was only a thirty-minute hike back to where the truck was parked. As she arrived, she noticed the absence of the vehicle and knew they were safe.

After a few seconds of waiting, a dust cloud headed up the road towards her. The sounds of the manual transmission fighting the climb came through the cloud. They'd been waiting around the bend to see who appeared within their extra spotting scope.

The dust had barely cleared when Abbie jumped free of the passenger door and rushed to Alma, hugging her over her rifle. Becca jogged around from the driver's side and embraced the two other women. They stood there, breathing together, trying to calm. Becca pulled away first, wiping tears from her eyes. "Gina?" she asked.

"It ripped off her head and took off after you two." Alma's voice sounded alien to her, like listening to a distorted recording.

"What?" Abbie dropped away from Alma and covered her mouth with her hands.

"Tore off her head?" Becca began the frantic breathing of an oncoming panic attack.

"We have to kill it." Alma turned from them to look back into the forest. "I think it's going to come back for us."

"Okay, okay," Abbie was nodding her head.

Becca stopped hyperventilating and screeched out, "we have to call the police! The forest service! Someone!" She immediately went back to her frantic-paced breathing.

Abbie kept nodding her head, "Okay, okay."

"Where's the satellite phone?" Alma's voice was cool and emotionless.

Becca produced it from her jacket pocket and handed it to Alma. Jorge had already saved the number of the nearest ranger station, which Alma found and dialed. Becca and Abbie could hear a cheerful male voice pick up on the other end. Alma told him a wild animal had attacked their friend and described their location. After reassuring him she understood, she hung up the phone. "He wants us to go down to the gate and wait for him there."

Becca nodded and took the phone back. She tucked it into her jacket pocket then went to get in the truck. Abbie followed her. Alma turned and started to walk into the woods. Becca yelled out, "what are you doing? Get in the car!"

Alma turned to face her again. "I have to. It's going to hunt us all down." She took another step into the woods.

"Alma!" Becca screamed, and the other two women froze. Her breathing had calmed, but her face was ashy, and distorted between fear and disgust.

Alma looked at her, waiting.

"We have to go drive by camp on the way to the gate. You need more ammo. I have Jorge's .38 there. Come back with us to camp. We'll get you loaded up, and then drop you off before we go to the gate, alright?"

Alma paused, head cocked to one side, considering, then nodded and went to climb into the back seat of the truck. Abbie exhaled a low sigh of relief and jumped into the passenger seat. Becca drove.

The carnage was visible a dozen yards before they reached camp. Remnants of gear and fabric were thrashed along the road, now streamers and confetti made from thousands of dollars in hunting and camping gear. They pulled up cautiously and lowered the windows to listen for sounds.

The day rang out with the normal joyous noises of forest birds chirping and occasional chipmunk chatter. Becca turned off the ignition and left the keys inside. They sat stone still, waiting, and unsure.

A huge tree branch flew at them from the front of the vehicle, shattering the windshield and impaling the back seat, inches from where Alma sat. The women screamed. A large thump, thump, thump came as the creature approached, each footstep an earthshaking drumbeat. It came from the left, grabbed onto the driver's side door, and ripped it free from the vehicle with a deafening crunch.

Becca reared back and began kicking at the beast as Alma tried to line up a shot. From the backseat of the truck with the branch blocking her view, there was no way to shoot without risking Becca. The beast grabbed Becca by the foot and yanked her free from the vehicle.

Abbie managed to get a hold of her door handle and opened it behind her, falling backwards out of the truck.

The beast held Becca up by the foot as she continued to swing at it and thrash. After inspecting her for a second, it grabbed her other foot and lifted her higher into the air. It started to pull her legs apart. Becca screamed louder.

Alma threw her door open and jumped down, almost landing on top of Abbie, who had been scooting backwards on her butt. Rounding the back of the truck, Alma lifted her AR to her shoulder as the beast came into view. Becca was still screaming as her pelvis split into two and one leg ripped free from the hip. Alma fired into the beast's chest.

The first shot made it step backwards and drop both sides of Becca to the ground. The second shot made it sway on the side it had been hit on. The third made it double over and roar in anger. The fourth shot jammed.

Alma held the rifle steady, the beast looked at her and roared again, then dropped to all four legs and galloped into the woods. Alma waited. It did not reappear.

Becca continued to scream, although the sound was becoming weaker. A lake of blood surrounded her. The injured woman babbled some nonsensical words and Alma nodded and shushed her, holding her tight. The noises quieted and stopped. Alma stared into the woods, rifle close by.

"Alma?" Abbie had crept around the side of the truck and saw Becca's body for the first time. "Oh God, oh God, oh God."

"Quiet." Alma hissed, "It's still out there. It's injured, and it's angry."

Abbie curled up next to the truck and rocked back and forth.

Alma reached into Becca's jacket pocket and found the satellite phone, warm from Becca's body heat. She tucked it inside her shirt, securing the large phone under her bra strap. "Abbie."

"Yeah?" Abbie's voice was weak, the audio version of a limp noodle.

"I need to clear a jam in the gun, alright? Can you watch the woods for me while I do that?

"Uh-huh."

Alma quickly removed the stuck bullet, thankful that even though Gauge had sent her with his janky homemade ammo, that he'd also taught her how to clear it. She ejected the magazine, inspected it, and reinserted. How many rounds would it take to get them out of the woods?

"Abbie," she called and heard a soft moan in response. "We need to check the camp, see if there's any of my bullets left, or any other guns. Okay?"

Abbie moaned something unintelligible and got to her feet. Alma slid Becca's head gently off her lap into the dirt. Aiming the barrel into the woods where it had galloped off, Alma stood up and began shuffling backwards into camp. "Search for things, while I watch the woods."

Abbie didn't respond but began poking through the remnants of their gear. She found some intact water bottles and placed them near Alma's feet.

"In the truck." Alma said without taking her eyes off the forest.

Abbie moved the items and continued searching. Soon after, she gave a small cry of victory and held up an intact and fully loaded extra magazine for Alma's rifle.

Alma heaved a smile out and motioned to bring it over where she shoved it into her pants pocket. Several minutes later Abbie had found the .38 revolver, four undamaged bullets for it, one unopened box of granola bars and another bottle of water. The two women stood alone in the trashed campsite. Abbie waiting expectantly for orders, Alma carefully sweeping the tree line across from them.

In her best church-quiet voice, Alma said, "I think the truck will still run; we're just going to have a tough time seeing through that windshield. If we can make it to the gate, the forest service and the police will be there. It won't be able to survive them. Okay?"

Abbie whispered back, "Okay."

"Pick up the .38 and load it and turn the chamber so it's ready to fire."

Abbie did as she was told and whispered, "Our rifles are still in the truck bed, Becca's and mine."

"Got it. Load them into the truck with the rest of the stuff with one hand, while keeping the .38 up with the other. I will cover you. Okay?"

Abbie had everything tucked away into the truck in seconds. She waited by the passenger door and nodded to Alma, using the pistol to sweep across the trees the way Alma had done.

Alma broke into a sprint and flew into the truck, making sure not to look at Becca's body again as she slid into the driver's seat. She heard the noise of Abbie climbing in beside her and started the truck as she heard the door shut.

The truck came alive without issue, and they started towards the gate. With the shattered windshield and dusty roads, Alma could only go around twenty miles per hour before visibility disappeared. They were only driving for a couple minutes when Abbie yelped, "It's behind us!"

In the rearview mirror, the beast had appeared a hundred yards back, limping, but relentless. Alma tried to speed up and the dust clouded around them, limiting their vision and making them cough. They rounded several bends and lost the beast for moments, but not for long before it reappeared in the distance. It grew larger in the mirror; it was gaining on them.

The road made a sharp right where it edged alongside a steep cliff face of the mountain. Alma had to slow down to make the turn without losing traction, and the beast grew larger. It roared and Abbie cried out. They safely made the turn and went about two hundred feet when Alma slammed on the brakes.

"Hey!" Abbie yelled, turning to her in a panic. "Go! Go!"

The beast appeared around the bend and began jogging towards the stopped vehicle. Alma put the truck in reverse and floored the pedal. The three hundred and sixty horsepower truck roared backwards and slammed into the beast, who was thrown forward onto the truck. It screamed in pain and surprise.

The trucked continued careening backwards towards the cliff edge. Alma looked at Abbie, "Jump!"

Both women jumped clear of the vehicle a second before it flew backwards off the cliff edge, disappearing from sight. A screaming roar sounded over the loud crunching of the truck, crumpling against the steep granite face.

Abbie yelped in pain as she got up from the ground. She had landed in the bushes and gotten scratched up. Her ankle was injured and pain shot through her every time she stepped down. "Alma?" she called out and limped over to the other side of the road.

To the left, the road was bordered by trees growing up from the steep cliff face, although not as steep as the side the truck had just gone over. Alma lay against a tree trunk a foot from the road, her eyes closed and unmoving. "Alma?" Abbie called again.

Alma groaned before speaking. "I think I broke my arm."

Abbie giggled hysterically and then blushed. "Come on." She got to her knees to help Alma up.

The two women helped each other walk to the edge where the truck had gone over. A twisted heap of metal lay smashed against a twenty-foot boulder, over a hundred feet below them. Blood decorated the cliff side all around it. A massive antler lay tangled in a bush a few feet away from the wreckage. The woman waited. No sound or movement appeared.

"Let's get going, just in case." Alma said and Abbie nodded in vigorous agreement. The two started down the mountain. Alma pulled the phone free from her bra and found it undamaged and functional. She called the ranger station again, who put her through to the officer waiting at the gate and let them know the truck had been wrecked. The officers agreed to break the lock and meet them as soon as possible. The women walked, limping, their arms around each other, Alma's injured arm tucked against her chest.

The dust kicking up before them brought joy and relief. Both women laughed, shouted, and let their legs give out. A police SUV and a ranger's truck stopped in front of them, and four men got out to rush to their aid. Alma and Abbie were each given water and were being helped to the vehicles when one of the men looked up the road at a sudden noise. "What in the hell is that?" he asked.

The Underground

"Are you ready? Here we go." Tyson hopped up from the bench they'd been waiting on while the rest of the group gathered and held his hand out to Margot.

A person dressed in skinny black jeans and a t-shirt was walking through the crowd, asking for tickets. They approached the couple. "Tickets please?"

Tyson opened his phone and pulled up the barcode he had saved. The person scanned it with their phone and continued on towards the next group.

Tyson snickered at Margot. "Was that a man or a woman?"

"Shut up Ty, we're in Portland." Margot swatted him on the arm. They'd had many talks about him being more tolerant. After all, he was the one who chose to relocate to the area. She'd told him repeatedly, "you can't move here and expect everyone else to change." He'd give a noncommittal grunt in response.

They'd been dating for three years and had driven over from Vancouver, where they lived. Margot worked as a diet aide at the local hospital. One day she had tripped and fell into Tyson, who was a new LPN. When she'd met him, his choice of profession had impressed her and she assumed him a considerate, empathetic person. Now there were times when she wondered why he continued to do this kind of work. To her, this trip was a last chance at rekindling their relationship. She'd moved into his apartment a year before. Things had only declined since then. They fought almost daily. Most days, she felt more like a nanny than she did his girlfriend. Between the messes, chores he didn't do, and his constant need for some kind of placating, sex had nearly evaporated from their lives.

The person in black headed to the front of the group and jumped onto a bench nearby. "Everyone, hello, I'm Pat, and it's nice to meet you all. A couple of reminders before we head into The Underground Tour. Number one: take as many pictures as you like, but please don't touch anything. Things are old, fragile, and authentic. You could get hurt. Number two: Stay together. We only have time to explore a short portion of the underground. It's easy to get lost, or worse. Number three: You may see, or be touched by rats, bats, spiders, worms, or any other kind of creepy crawlies. It's their home you're in. Please do not panic or attack anything. Lastly: if you get claustrophobic, or are faint of heart, let someone know right away if you need to get out. We have emergency shortcuts we can use if anyone isn't feeling well. Questions?"

Tyson leaned into Margot's ear. "Well, that cleared up

nothing."

She responded by lightly stepping on his toes.

"What?" Tyson hissed. "You like him or something? Maybe you should go give him your number and I'll go hit up the club."

Margot rolled her eyes. One of the most exhausting things about him was his constant jealousy. She couldn't even grab a cup of coffee with her sister without him wanting to check her phone.

An older couple at the front needed some help with their phones. While they waited, a nervous excitement built in the air. At last, the group surged forward, following Pat into the side of an ancient brick building.

There were at least twenty people on this tour. A motley crew of typical tourists. Enough people that the couple could blend into the background and continue to banter quietly while the guide narrated the journey.

This was their last stop before heading home and closing out the weekend. The previous two days had been tense. The couple had argued about everything from where they ate to how fast they would get there. Margot had been ready to call it good when she woke up that morning, but Tyson had insisted on this last stop. He'd surprised her by saying he'd already bought tickets in advance and texting them to her, something not like him.

Another tour guide had joined them. A woman in a pirate-style outfit and a booming voice took over inside a dark room filled with glass cabinets. She walked around and explained the history of the objects on display and where they were originally found along the tour. Tyson stifled a yawn while Margot strained to hear every detail.

The pirate woman's voice was loud, but lyrical. "The underground is bigger than we know. It stretches for many blocks on the waterfront, connecting the basements of several of the buildings you still see standing. Since much of it has not been explored because of legal and safety reasons, it is very important to stay with the group."

When the woman had finished talking, the group followed her outside and down an alleyway, before entering another basement door. "Keep close everyone," Pat called out. "This is a direct entrance to where the tunnels used to be. Make sure you stay together."

They walked through a room with narrow bunk beds set against the walls. The pirate woman told the group. "Here are the remnants of a real-life opium den. People could be down here for hours, or days. And if someone couldn't pay their bill…" She lifted a hatch in the floor, and everyone gathered around. "Shanghaied!"

The uncovered hole in the ground disappeared into blackness. Margot felt a chill squirm down her shoulders, and she shivered.

"What?" Tyson pinched her side. "You afraid I'm gonna throw you down there?"

"Shut up, Ty." Margot moved away from him, across the room.

At the far wall, she turned around to stare at the opium den again. The idea of self-drugged men and women wasting their lives, laying in those bunks sickened her.

"It's really something, isn't it?" An old woman to her left asked, eyes wide.

"Chilling." Margot agreed. She raised her phone and snapped a few pictures.

They followed the tour guides through to another room. In each space, they had stopped to share stories about the history or claimed hauntings. Tyson responded to each with a snort or clearing his throat or some other skeptical noise.

"Shhh." Margot nudged him. "I really want to hear this."

Tyson shrugged and wandered off.

Margot continued to take pictures. Away from the group, she stopped to review her footage. The first few pictures captured the gloom well enough, but didn't fully encompass the dire feeling of the space. The last picture of the opium den made her pause. In the center of the photo, right in the middle of the room, stood a young man smiling at the camera.

"What the?" she said and zoomed in. He looked to be around twenty-one years old. Handsome, he had a wide, bright smile and was wearing a navy peacoat with both hands shoved in the pockets, as though reluctant to pose. Margot swiped to the next photo. It showed the same space and angle, but no people in the image. She swiped back to the smiling man.

The young man's face was a combination of apologetic and prankster. The man winked. Margot yelped and dropped the phone.

Tyson's head jerked up at the noise and he came rushing over. "Mar? What's wrong?"

Margot found her phone and stood up, thumbing open the welcome screen. "There was this guy in one of my pics and it looked like the picture winked at me."

"You took a pic of some dude winking at you?" His voice had become louder, edged with threat.

"No! no, I took a photo of that room, the opium den, and some guy photo bombed me."

"Well, where is he? I'll tell him he can't do that."

The two of them scanned the group. "He's not here." Margot whispered.

"Look." Tyson pulled her to the other side of the room. They ducked behind a wall, out of direct sight from the others. "Why the fuck are you taking pictures of other men?"

"I'm not, I didn't."

"Show me. Show me the photo."

Margot tried to pull up the images on her phone. At a distance, they heard Pat call out that it was time to leave. Shuffling feet and quiet murmurs began to fade as the group reversed their course. She thumbed back and forth through the photos. "It's gone." She looked up into his eyes. "It's gone. I don't know what happened."

"You deleted it."

"No! It's just gone."

Tyson grabbed her by the arm and pulled her further back into the space, away from the others. "You know Margot, the whole reason I brought you on this stupid tour was because I was gonna propose to you at the end. You know that?" His voice was a violent, sharp hiss.

"What?"

"Shut up. I was gonna finally propose and instead you're out here taking pictures of other dudes. You know what Margot? Fuck you." Tyson took a small box out of his pocket and then chucked it into the blackness of the area behind them.

"Tyson, no."

"Shut up, Margot. Just shut up." Tyson stepped back and glanced behind him. No one from their tour group remained in eyesight. "Just shut the fuck up. Slut." With both hands, he shoved her backwards, hard, then turned and strode away.

Margot shrieked as she fell into the dark. Her body landed on a layer of musty canvas which had covered a kidnapping pit. The fabric loosened and slipped, not being secured to anything. She fell inside, the fabric enveloping her. Seconds passed, an eternity of floating, before crashing into something hard. She fought the canvas until wrenching it free from her face. Darkness surrounded her.

"Tyson!" she screamed.

Tyson rushed through the empty rooms and emerged from the entryway into a small courtyard where everyone else was collected.

"Are you the last one out?" Pat asked, holding a padlock.

"Yup, yes. Last one." Tyson sputtered the words and pushed through the crowd towards the exit. Outside, he looked around before landing his eyes on a quaint café nearby. There were a few empty tables out front, and the door was jammed open with a small statue of a dragon. He jogged over, and laughed to himself, thinking how pissed Margot would be getting stuck in there for a few hours. Worst case scenario, she'd be trapped until the next tour started later that day. She'd be scared shitless wandering in the dark. Fucking bitch deserved it, taking pictures of other men.

Inside the cafe, he startled the barista, wheezing from his jog across the street. "Bathroom key," he blurted out.

The barista raised one eyebrow and handed him a card on a long, rainbow-colored lanyard. He tripped, stumbled, and swore, trying to move as fast as possible. Inside the bathroom was a single toilet and sink in a small, lockable room. A short bookcase held some cleaning supplies and extra toilet paper. Behind him, a narrow closet door looked older than the building and sat at an awkward angle within the frame.

At the sink, he splashed cool water onto his face. "Stupid dumb slut," he mumbled, drinking slurps from the running faucet. The lights flickered and went out.

"Hey!" he shouted and whirled to slap at the wall where the light switch should be. After a couple of tries, his fingers found the plastic and flipped it. The room illuminated and standing in front of the door was the corpse of a man wearing a navy pea coat. His eyes were rotted out and his skin eaten away in patches, revealing white bone underneath. The corpse appeared to be smiling, or that may have been the result of him missing most of his lips.

The gap around the mouth widened. "Hey." It responded.

Tyson shrieked. He lunged for the closet door, and the knob turned in his hands. It opened to darkness, and he bolted inside, falling through a hole in the floor. He landed hard on his butt and fell backwards, cracking his skull on the concrete ground of the basement at the bottom of the ladder he hadn't seen. The world dimmed and went dark.

Above him, the bathroom was empty. A knock came from the door. The concerned barista. "Mister, are you okay? I heard a scream."

A few seconds passed. The barista knocked again. "Mister? You better not be doing drugs in there."

The barista pulled a key from their pocket and inserted it into the door, bypassing the card reader. Inside the bathroom looked undisturbed, although a few drops of water clung to the side of the sink. Confused, they scratched their face and shook their head, then shrugging, went back to work.

A Good Prank

It was a perfect day for a hike. The snow had receded now that spring was nearing, and it was supposed to be clear and sunny out. The group still brought rain gear and dressed in layers for the fifty-degree weather. The conditions could turn faster than you realized, and it was always better to be prepared.

Amy, Evan, Tristan, Leigh, Zane, and Max stood in a semicircle, waiting for Tristan's new girlfriend, Tiên. Everyone except her had been lifelong friends. They were all in college, although not all the same school. Getting out for weekend hikes was one of the ways the friend group had stayed in contact with each other. Tiên appeared out of thin air in the parking lot, boots crunching on gravel as she walked.

"Hi, I'm here!" She called out and rushed over, apologizing repeatedly for being late.

No problem, they reassured her. Plenty of time still left in the day.

"Oh! I need to text my sister." Leigh said, typing furiously into her phone.

Tiên waited with a puzzled look on her face.

Leigh finished and looked up. "Before each hike, I tell her where I'm going, what I'm wearing, and who I'm with. Just in case."

"Is it gonna be dangerous?" Tiên asked.

"No, no, no," Max told her. "It's just in case. In the off chance something happens, we'll be easier to find. But nothing will happen."

"Oh!" Leigh said. I didn't mention you were here, Tiên. But you told someone right? That you were going hiking?"

"Um, yes." Tiên looked at Tristan, who smiled at her and squeezed her shoulder.

"This is her first hike," Tristan told the group. "She thinks forests are kind of spooky."

The friends laughed and reassured her that this would be a breeze.

They began the ascent. The trail they'd chosen was remote and not popular. It had gorgeous views of the mountains and giant, cascading waterfalls, but the path consisted of a near constant staircase-like climb. The edges of the path razor backed up the sheer granite mountain face and frequently had sharp drop-offs, several hundred feet to the ground below. Each viewpoint was a jagged edge of bare flat rock, sticking out perilously into the air. This trail had no guardrails the way some of the more popular ones did. The pictures would be amazing, but the combination of brutal climb and risky falls kept most people away.

Still in their early twenties, and in good shape, everyone felt well equipped to handle the intensity of the trail. During the initial climb, they basked in the quiet, soft noises of the forest. Each of them worked to find their breath among this pathway so steep that it reduced them to bouldering in places. They soon reached a flatter section, where a few large rocks sat, spread around. A good spot to hydrate and rest for a moment.

"This trail is brutal," Evan said, and poured drops of water over his face.

"It's actually not even on the maps anymore." Zane told him and pulled the bottle from his hands before taking a swig and handing it back. "They stopped maintaining it because it was too steep towards the top. We might have to turn around if it's washed out anywhere."

Tiên looked up at Tristan. "Why are we doing this one if it could be washed out?"

"Because!" Amy jumped up and clapped her hands. "The waterfalls we're going to see are spectacular!"

"You're in a good mood today," Leigh told her, raising her eyebrows.

Zane walked over to Amy and pretended to use her head as an arm rest. "That's because she's not the only tiny Asian in the circle now!"

Amy ducked away and swatted at him. "Not funny, Zane."

"I'm just saying. If you keep disappearing on us, maybe we'll need to replace you."

Leigh tossed a pebble at him. "Bad joke, Zane. You're making Tiên not like us and then Tristan will be single until he dies."

"It's fine." Tiên stood up from the rock she'd been sitting on and smiled. "Are we ready to go?"

The group soldiered on. The climb became less intense, but

still a workout. They huffed along and the conversation stayed at a minimum. Several times the lip of the trail cut to a steep drop off, and they fell into single file to avoid risking going over. Close to the two-mile mark, Leigh squealed and pointed. "The first waterfall lookout!" She rushed ahead.

In front of them was a giant flat rock, worn free of moss and debris. The far corner narrowed into a jagged point, lifting out of the trees. One by one, they took turns walking out as far as they dared to see the thundering falls from the mid-way point. Below them, a deep green, clear pool of water surrounded the turbulent base. Above them, the waterfall lifted impossibly close to the sky. The scene was breathtaking, and the friends stood still, inhaling the mist and enjoying the moment.

On the wider parts of the rock, the group rested, drank water and talked while they went one by one to take in the view better.

Leigh sat down next to Tiên. "So, how did you and Tristan meet?"

Tiên blushed; she wasn't used to talking about herself. "Um, at the library. We were at the same study table, and I asked if he wanted to get some coffee with me."

"Nice, Tris." Leigh winked at him. "Good job, Mr. smooth talker."

Tristan shrugged and smiled apologetically.

Tiên's blush bloomed deeper across her face. "How did all of you meet?"

Everyone had finished their time with the waterfall and was now gathered in a circle on the rock, hydrating and snacking. They all looked to each other to see who would start the story.

"I guess it started with us," Evan said and squeezed Zane's knee. We met in kindergarten and immediately became inseparable.

Zane laughed. "The only two gay kids in the entire grade ended up in the same room together. We had to be besties."

Evan batted his eyes. "Love at first sight."

"You're dating?" Tiên asked.

The group exploded into laughter.

"Off and on." Zane pulled Evan in for a hug. "This bitch can never get away from me."

"For life." Evan added and kissed him on the cheek.

"But not right now."

"No, now we're just taking things as they come."

"Oh, okay." Tiên smiled at the goofy pair. Now play wrestling. "But, how about everyone else?"

Zane threw a pinecone at Leigh's feet. "Well, she's my fag hag."

Leigh kicked it back. "Oh my God, Zane, stop calling me that."

Evan reached over, picked up the pinecone and threw it at Tristan. "And I tried to date this bitch, but he's sadly with the straights."

Tristan shrugged again. "But I introduced you to Max, who you did date." He turned to Tiên. "Max and I were friends for years from soccer, but it was clear early on he swung both ways."

"Oh." Tiên couldn't stop the blushing, and it got worse the more everyone talked. Her face felt swollen. "So Evan has dated both Max and Zane?"

"And I've dated Max." Leigh interrupted, "but not for long. We're one of those typical half-incestuous friend groups."

Everybody except Tiên laughed, and they collectively got to their feet.

"Onward!" Evan sang and darted up the path, quickly

disappearing from sight.

They fell into line and plodded after. The way switchbacked and would meander between steep steps carved into the mountain's granite or long narrow slopes with random dips or hills. For a while, the only sounds were the vibrant forest and the huffing of the college students trying to catch their breath while they kept up the pace.

The route dropped into a wider, relaxed track as it neared the next viewing point. The sounds of everyone panting diminished.

"Hey." Tiên stalled and swiveled. "Where's Amy?"

The party halted and searched around them. Amy had disappeared.

Leigh was at the front of the line. "I don't think she's ahead of us, but I could be wrong. I was pretty focused on making it up that last slope. Maybe she stopped to pee?"

Everyone scanned each other's faces for answers. Several non-committal noises were made.

"Wouldn't she have said something?" Tiên asked.

"Oh no." Max laughed. "She disappears like that all the time. She'd just up and disappear from parties and stuff. We stopped questioning it years ago. We hadn't even heard from her in six months before today."

"Oh." Tiên fidgeted with her hands. "You never said how you met Amy?"

Leigh, Evan, Zane, Max, and Tristan shared a look back and forth amongst them.

Tristan broke the silence. "I guess we met her in middle school."

Zane laughed. "Do you guys remember how mad she used to get about her name?"

Evan and Max guffawed, while Tristan and Leigh giggled; a nervous undercurrent running through it.

"Her name?" Tiên asked, eyebrows raised.

"Oh God." Evan wiped his eyes. "I forgot." He laughed again. "Her name technically isn't Amy. Our teachers couldn't say her name right. They kept calling her Amy, and she'd get so mad. Once she screamed and threw a pencil at the teacher. It was so fucking funny."

"But you guys call her Amy?"

"Yeah." Zane shrugged. "She'd get so freaking mad, all the students started calling her Amy too. Eventually she got over it and accepted her name is Amy now." He giggled again, a shrill noise that reminded Tiên of the chipmunks they'd heard during the hike.

"Well, what's her real name?"

"Something that sounds like Amy."

Leigh smacked Zane on the arm. "Her name was Anh Lệ, but now she just goes by Amy." Leigh lifted her arms, palms turned upward and shrugged. "Amy fits. She's an Amy. She just didn't know it yet."

"Heeyyyyy you guys!" Amy's voice boomed from above them. "Are you coming?"

Everyone turned to look ahead. A few hundred feet away, at the next bend, stood Amy, waving madly.

Evan cupped his hands around his mouth. "WE THOUGHT YOU WERE PEEING."

Amy waved them towards her and disappeared behind the trees. The group trudged on.

Soon, the next viewpoint came into sight. Jutting out over the sky was a large rocky platform, just off the path. Amy was at the edge, standing with her arms spread wide, as though she were preparing to swan dive off.

"Wait!" Zane yelled, "Don't jump! You have so much to live for!" And laughed at his own joke.

Amy turned and waved again. They caught up and

encircled her, looking over into a stunning view of the same waterfall they'd seen earlier, but from a much better lookout.

Wiggling her fingers out in front of her, Amy asked, "don't you ever feel like if you wished hard enough, you could fly? You could just fly away?"

Leigh tugged on Amy's shirt, pulling her backwards. "Ok, yes, but maybe let's not test that here."

"Not me." Max swished some water in his mouth and spat. "I'd wish to be a billionaire."

"Spiderman." Evan and Zane said simultaneously, laughing. "Jinx!" They said and laughed again.

"No world peace?" Leigh asked, raising one eyebrow. "Oh, okay then. Selfish cunts."

"Don't lie Leigh. You don't want world peace. What would you really wish for?" Max spat again, this time landing the wad inches from Leigh's shoes.

She shot him a smirk. "OK, honestly, I've thought about this a lot and I'd want the ability to speak, read, and understand every language that has ever existed."

Tristan let out a low whistle. "That's pretty noble, Leigh. I'd just want money. Lots of money. I'm with Zane."

"Oh, you're with me now?" Zane winked at Tristan.

"I'd want the power to make world peace." Tiên said, louder than she intended.

They turned to regard her.

"Like, if I were a world leader, like the president. Maybe I could make peace. Make people be good to each other somehow. Or maybe I'd just wish for people to be good to each other."

Tristan kissed her on the top of her head. "That's really sweet Tiên. I like it."

Tiên's face had calmed but now flamed pink again. She'd been blushing so hard today that she felt almost feverish.

"Hey." Zane pulled his backpack straps tight. "I gotta go take a piss. I'll be right back." He turned and jogged up the trail.

"Guess we're waiting here then." Tristan sat down and leaned back against a tree.

Tiên sat next to him. "You guys still never said how you started hanging out with Amy, just that you met her in middle school."

"Tristan didn't tell you?" Amy asked, now sitting, but still precariously close to the hundred-foot fall.

Tiên glanced at Tristan for an explanation, but he refused to make eye contact with her, staring into the sky instead.

"We dated." Amy said. "We dated and broke up, but I kept hanging around their friend group for some weird reason."

"Um," Leigh said, "because we love you! Because you were so much fun to have around. We're not gonna dump someone we love just because of a little breakup."

"I didn't realize I was so fun. I thought Zane and Max were the fun ones." Amy used her finger to draw in the dust on the rock face. "I thought you all just liked watching me react."

Silence overcame them, no one wanting to meet another's eyes. Tiên surveyed the friends and waited for an explanation.

Leigh reached over and squeezed Amy's knee. "We like you, just as you are. I'm glad you came today."

Amy snorted and stared at her drawing on the ground. It was a large spiral, with clouds and symbols around it in various places.

Evan clapped his hands together. "Zane should have been back by now. It's been like ten minutes."

"Maybe he's taking a shit?" Max got to his feet and dusted off his pants.

Tristan rolled his eyes. Leigh, Amy, and Tiên blanched in

disgust.

"I don't think so." Evan was oblivious to the group's collective gross-out. "He shit this morning before we left the apartment. My phone says it can't send any texts."

"Yeah." Leigh checked her phone, getting ready to go. "There's, like, almost no service up here. Some parts of the mountain get it though. Let's go find him. Make sure he didn't find a cougar or something."

"Come on, Leigh." Max poked her in the ribs. "We're hiking, not in a dive bar."

Leigh tossed her ponytail and pushed past him. "Amy, come walk with me. Let's catch up. It's been forever, girl." Leigh stopped, confused. "Amy?"

Amy had gone missing. Everyone began to look around, calling "Amy?" into the air.

Tristan's and Evan's eyes met. Together they took several, tentative steps towards the edge of the cliff that Amy had been sitting near. Tristan reached over and grabbed Evan's hand. Evan took a step back and braced himself while Tristan leaned over the ledge and looked down. Leigh, Tiên, and Max held their breath, frozen in place.

After scanning the landscape, Tristan declared. "She's not there."

A collective "phew" went around and they resumed looking for her.

Seconds later, Amy emerged from behind a tree. "Sorry, sorry everyone. Had to pee, too. I didn't think you'd notice."

"Oh my God, Amy." Leigh reached out for her. "Don't scare me like that, we can't have two people go missing."

Amy murmured "sorry" again and rushed to catch up to Leigh.

The party marched quietly, except for one of them calling for Zane every few seconds. Once, a bird responded with a shrill squawk that startled everyone, followed by nervous laughter. They approached a fork in the trail.

"Ah shit." Max jumped onto a rock and tried to see around them from his slightly higher position. "Now what?"

Leigh pulled out her phone and opened her notes for the hike. "Left is the trail to the summit. Right is some kind of side trail to another viewpoint. Let's split up. Whoever goes to the top can wait until the rest catch up."

"Max and I can do the side trail." Evan volunteered. "It's leg day, goddammit."

"I'll join you, if that's alright?" Amy asked, hands shoved in her pockets, looking down at her shoes.

"Of course, girl!" Evan grabbed the hem of her shirt and tugged her forward. "Let's Jane Fonda that ass!"

"Who?" Amy pushed him away and started towards the other path.

"Never mind." Evan cupped his hands around his mouth. "Zane!" He yelled as he walked. Max joined him and the two took turns calling for Zane as they moved away from the group, Amy following behind.

Leigh, Tristan, and Tiên walked up the other trail, also shouting for Zane periodically. They quickly ran out of the ability to yell while hiking up the steep incline. After a half mile, they reached a smaller, less exciting view of the falls.

"Zane had to have gone up the other trail." Leigh said between sips off her water bottle. "There's no way he walked this far just to pee."

"So, what should we do?" Tiên's face was knotted in concern.

"Keep going. The others will probably find him, lost, on that side trail. We can slow down and give them a chance to catch up before we reach the top. It's fine. Zane's a joker. This is probably just another one of his stupid pranks."

"Oh." Tiên scuffed her shoe in the dirt. "Is that what Amy meant by 'watching her react?'"

"Uh, yeah, I guess." Leigh walked from the small viewpoint to the trail. "Let's keep going. I want to get home today in time to get some studying done."

The trio moved away from the view and kept on towards the summit.

"What kinds of pranks did he play on her?"

Neither Tristan nor Leigh replied. Tristan cleared his throat.

"Well?" Tiên asked, looking back at Tristan.

His neck flushed up to his ears. "Amy was really jumpy when we were younger. So, Zane loved to scare her all the time. He'd jump out from behind stuff. Sometimes wearing a mask. He put a giant spider on her once."

"A fake spider?"

"No, a wolf spider the size of his hand. I'm still shocked he had the balls to pick it up."

"Jesus…"

Tristan stopped walking and pulled Tiên to him. "Look, I want you to know that we all feel really bad about it now. We didn't all do stuff to her, but we let it happen. After the last time, we sat those guys down and had a conversation about it. Things should be cool. They won't pull that shit again."

Tiên looked to Leigh, who looked away and kept hiking.

Tristan was smiling at her, awaiting a response.

"Okay." Tiên said and smiled at him. His eyes were pleading with her to drop the subject. He let go of her and they hurried after Leigh.

The three of them reached a place on the trail where it became so narrow that they had to walk single file again. On one side, the trail abruptly dropped off into a cliff face. The trees soared above their heads. It was impossible to feel anything but insignificant next to the silent giants. Tiên peered over the edge; the drop was at least fifty feet down, further in places. Beneath them lay a boulder field, interspersed with the firs and cedars that towered up and away, shading the entire area. Massive ferns decorated the boulders, hiding many of the smaller rocks. Ahead of them, the trees fell away from the trail, making a sunny, bald spot marring the mountain.

Tristan was kicking small rocks over the cliff's rim, waiting until he heard a thunk before throwing another. "Who invited Amy anyhow? I thought she wasn't talking to us anymore."

"Um, not me." Leigh turned to face them. "I was afraid to offer that olive branch. It must have been either Zane or Max. One of them had to have apologized for real. I can't see her wanting to come back otherwise."

"I don't know what they could have said. I wouldn't have forgiven them."

"Yeah." Leigh stopped and took a drink of water. "I'd been wanting to reach out to her, but I figured it was better to give her space."

Tristan nodded in agreement. "Probably for the best."

They continued to hike up the mountain. Tiên walked in silence, questions swirling in her mind. She didn't want to ask. She knew she probably shouldn't ask. She blurted out, "What happened the last time? The time you all talked about it after?"

"Uuhhhh." Tristan dragged the word out as though he'd forgotten how to speak.

"They made her eat cum," Leigh said.

"What?"

Leigh let out a frustrated groan. "Zane, and I think Max maybe too. We were all drinking at Max's house, and Amy had decided she wanted some clam chowder. She was fall-down drunk, and Zane said he'd make it for her. I guess the guys went into the kitchen and jacked off into a bowl, poured the soup in and heated it up. She was like, absolutely shitfaced drunk."

They had stopped walking. Tiên looked incredulously from Leigh to Tristan.

Tristan grabbed Tiên by the shoulder. "It wasn't that bad. It sounds worse than it was."

"For fuck's sake, Tristan." Leigh closed her eyes. "They were all standing around, laughing at her while she ate it. They filmed it. It was fucking horrible. Zane called her a cum guzzling slut, and she was so drunk, she laughed at him."

Leigh bent over, hands resting on her knees, hair hanging over her face. "Tristan and I didn't find out until after, when they wouldn't stop laughing and rewatching the video. It was the grossest thing I've ever seen."

"She didn't have to know. She wouldn't have known if no one had sent it to her."

"One of you assholes uploaded to the internet! It was on at least three different apps. How was she not going to find out?"

"Hey, it wasn't me! I didn't do that."

"Tristan." Leigh stood, and was staring him down. Her nose was wrinkled, and teeth bared from her lip curled back.

"We all owe her an apology, okay? Let's just finish this hike and we can take her out, apologize, make things right and never bring this up again. Alright?"

Leigh shook her head and resumed marching. She reached the bald spot on the hillside, and her phone chirped with notifications. "You guys keep walking; I'm going to see if they found Zane."

Tiên squeezed by Leigh on the narrow trail, followed by

Tristan. He gave Leigh a wink as he slid past her body, rubbing against her to not teeter over into the abyss. She huffed and looked away, noticing Tiên catch the exchange.

Tiên turned and kept walking, hugging herself, arms wrapped tightly, despite the intense workout.

Leigh unlocked her phone and saw a new text from her sister. "Hey L, how are you hiking with Amy?"

She glared at the screen, difficult to read in the bright sun, and typed her response. "What do you mean? Yes, Amy is hiking with us."

Her sister sent a link to a news article. Leigh tapped on it. A new tab opened to an obituary titled "Young Woman Lost To Suicide." A picture of Amy graduating high school was underneath the headline, with a note stating the date the photo was taken. The article went on to explain that the young woman, Anh Le Ngoc, had taken her own life and was survived by her parents, younger sister, and grandparents, who had emigrated after the Vietnam war. It went on to describe Amy's hobbies and school performance.

Another text followed the link. "I thought you knew. I hadn't said anything before because I didn't want to upset you. Is that really Amy?"

Leigh shoved her phone in her pocket. "HEY," she yelled, "we need to go back!"

"What's going on?" Tiên asked.

"This is crazy, but my sister just told me Amy's supposed to be dead. We gotta go find the others."

Tristan jogged back to Leigh. "What?"

Leigh pulled her phone out, unlocked it, and handed it to him.

Tristan gasped. "What the fuck? We need to go back right now. There's no way that wasn't Amy."

"I know." Leigh zoomed in on the photo. "Is this some

kind of weird hoax? A prank?"

"Pretty good fucking prank. Let's just go." Tristan started to push past Leigh again, leaning close into her body.

"Stop!" Leigh yelled and pushed back against Tristan. He jumped back in surprise and wobbled towards the edge.

He started to go over, unable to balance, when Tiên came up behind him and grabbed him by his backpack. He exhaled a sigh of relief. "Holy shit, thank you Tiên, you just…"

Tiên shoved him hard, and he disappeared over the side. His body hit against the trees as it fell, shaking the branches.

Leigh screamed.

Tiên walked up to her. "Shh, shhh."

While Leigh continued to scream, Tiên raised her hand. She was holding a large rock, with the sharp edge pointed out. Tiên brought it down hard onto Leigh's forehead. The wound stunned her into silence. She stood, astonished, unmoving, while the bright sunlight streamed through the green foliage around them. A thick drop of blood appeared where the rock had broken skin. It ran down her nose and onto her cheek. Leigh reached up to wipe her face and saw her hand come away covered in blood. She screamed again.

Tiên raised the rock and hit her again, and again. Leigh continued to make a screaming noise, though it had become choked and gargle. She fell to her knees. Tiên grabbed her by the arm and pulled her towards the edge.

Leigh stopped screaming and chanted, "no, no, no, no, no…"

Tiên shoved her over, feeling gravity take control, and collapsed to the ground, huffing from the exertion. She could hear low moaning coming from the bottom of the drop off. The only other noise was an angry chipmunk chattering nearby. Tiên wondered if their bodies had knocked it out of it's tree and felt bad, pressing her fingers to her forehead. She took a drink of water, got up, dusted herself off and headed down the mountain.

A mile away, Amy, Evan, and Max had reached the end of the side trail. Like many of the other viewpoints, it ended in an overhanging cliff, allowing those brave enough to have a bird's eye view of the surrounding valley. Zane's water bottle was resting on the ground near the rim.

"Fuuuuu…" Evan said, voice trailing off.

"It'd be like him to want to pee off it." Max moved closer to the rock, searching the ground, but not looking over.

"Here," Evan said, reaching out a hand. "I can't look. If I see him, I'm going to die, I'm just going to die." He took a deep breath and yelled for Zane again.

Max slapped his hand away and walked closer to the edge. "I'm gonna look. Okay? I'm looking." Holding one arm behind him like a counter-weight, Max leaned out over the precipice. "Oh fuck. He's down there. Zane!" Max screamed. "Zane!"

Evan rushed over "Zane! Oh my God. Are you okay? Zane, say something!"

Amy walked up behind them. "Hey guys?"

"Amy! Go get help! Run to where there's cell reception and call 911!"

"Hey. Look at me though."

"What Amy?" Max and Evan both turned to look at her.

Evan wiped his eyes. "What, what is it?"

Amy smiled. "Boo." She said and shoved them both off the rock.

They screamed as they fell and stopped abruptly as they hit the ground, several stories below.

Amy was still smiling as she began walking back down the trail.

At the fork, Tiên was waiting for her. The two women

embraced, and spun, hugging, now crying.

"I did it." Tiên told her. "You can rest now."

Amy pulled away and wiped tears from her eyes. "Thank you."

Tiên brushed off her own tears. "Uh huh."

Amy leaned forward and kissed the wetness from Tiên's cheeks. "Take care of mom and dad, okay?"

Tiên nodded, the lump in her throat too large to do more.

Amy kissed her sister on the forehead and walked directly into the trees lining the path. She disappeared into the woods before anything else could be said.

Tiên wiped her face again and started the journey down. She had to get Amy's car away from the trailhead before anyone noticed the missing students. It was a long drive home, and she hated being out here alone. The forest, after all, spooked her.

Potluck

The dinner was an annual tradition. The family's own special brand of holiday. It happened in March, at the end of winter. When Chloe was little, she thought the yearly gathering was for someone's birthday. Later, as a teenager, it dawned on her while helping her mother make their signature dish; no one even had a birthday that month. She shrugged it off as being one of those things unique to her family, something that outsiders wouldn't understand.

It was a good test for new partners of family members. They'd meet everyone. The group would wait anxiously to see if the newcomer would politely try every dish or if they would balk at any. The dishes had a purpose. Someone who wasn't willing to embrace family traditions would not work out. Chloe was technically an adult now. At eighteen, she was finally able to participate in the entire meal. If she did well, she might someday make her own recipe, and get her own wishes granted. "Chop the cabbage finer." Her mother, Rutina, pointed at her from her own cutting board. "We want it to melt into the rice."

"Yes, Mother." Chloe turned the cutting board and diced the cabbage finer with her large butcher knife. The knife was a family heirloom of German steel, used for this preparation since before Chloe was born. Their dish was a general well-wishing for the entire family. Most of the dishes brought were for more specific wishes. Sometimes, if the recipe was perfect, a wish was granted right away. A failed wish meant a change was needed in the recipe or an attempt at something else. No one liked a failed recipe, but everyone knew the perfect recipe existed to grant any wish. They'd all seen proof of that.

In her household, finely chopped cabbage was mixed in with black beans and rice as part of a casserole. These ingredients brought wealth, luck, health, and fertility. The entire mixture was stirred into a special sauce and baked until set. They had it every year, with no changes. She finished chopping the cabbage and went to check the rice. It was perfect, fluffy, and light. It would bake well. Next, she checked the beans, cooked, and drained, they were also ready. Rutina finished chopping ingredients for the meaningless salad, which would be served to the children if they wouldn't eat any of the important dishes. She set the knife down carefully and went to stir her sauce.

The sauce was cream based, started with a roux. The fat used was pure lard from the annual butchering, then extra fine flour, and then cream. A dab of homemade bouillon, a large helping of sautéed minced garlic, salt, pepper, and a teaspoon of onion jam. Homemade onion jam, of course. Then came the second-to-last ingredient. Chloe watched out of the corner of her eye, pretending not to notice, even though she always had. Her mother took a special spoon out of the drawer. It was very long, and had a small, rounded spatula head. The edges were dulled. Rutina lifted her skirt and inserted the spoon between her legs. She twisted and wiggled it for a few seconds, then removed the device and stirred it into the sauce.

"The women of our family are why we've always been and will always be so blessed." She spoke the words with her back to Chloe. She'd said them every year since Chloe began helping her.

"Yes, mother." Chloe wrung her hands and pulled at her sleeves, then tugged her dress down and patted it into place. What sacrifice would her own wish require?

"Do you want to provide the drop?"

Chloe nodded and came over to where her mother stood, one hand held out in offering. She could always be counted on to contribute to her family. She was not a weak-minded person who recoiled at doing her duty.

Rutina pulled a safety pin from her pocket and carefully held Chloe's finger over the pot. One quick poke and a fat drop of blood appeared on the tip. She didn't wince anymore. The first time, she had been told this needed to be a willing gift. It was an honor to provide it. Rutina turned Chloe's hand over and squeezed. The drop fell into the sauce. After stirring, Rutina mixed everything in the casserole pan and placed it gently into the waiting oven.

The doorbell rang and both women looked up. Rutina wrinkled her nose. "Someone is early."

"I've got it, mother." Chloe smiled and went to answer the door.

She opened it to find her Uncle Bart and Aunt Evelynn greeting her in unison. "Chloe!" They cheered, speaking over each other about how healthy she looked and how tall she'd become, despite being the same height as last year. She flinched at their grasping. Aunt Evelynn held up her pie, served every year, although a little different each time. "I brought the pie!"

"Wonderful," Chloe gave her aunt a quick side hug before taking the dish out of her hands. "May this year find you fecund."

Uncle Bart squeezed her shoulder, "Thank you, sweetie. I really think this will be our year."

Chloe followed them into the house and set the pie on the buffet, where it would soon be joined by single cousin Liberty's rose, strawberry, and beef heart cobbler. Another dessert would join the offerings this year, but it hadn't arrived yet.

Uncle Bart and Aunt Evelynn's pie was a custard-based dish, made with a dozen eggs. The yolks went into the filling, and the whites made the meringue on top. They had been trying for a baby for the last 8 years. Chloe knew that as an adult, she'd be expected to take and eat a slice of the pie. This wasn't her first time trying it. She'd snatched a bite off her mother's plate the first year they tried. She hadn't liked it then. It was too salty, the meringue too slimy. The custard smelled faintly of unwashed body, underneath the sweetness. She took a deep breath and exhaled slowly through her nose at the thought. They changed the recipe each year, trying to find the right ingredients, maybe it tasted better now. Chloe squared her shoulders. Everyone had to be all in, or the magic wouldn't work. There was no skipping dishes or politely hiding your serving under a napkin.

Rutina joined them with a bottle of wine and a couple of

glasses.

"Hello, sister." She said and kissed Evelynn on the cheek. "The pie again," she murmured, and Evelynn shot her a look. Both women had lamented many times about their inability to find the right ingredients to make the perfect dish. The one that would finally bring a new baby. The special magic that would change everything. That was the first part, anyhow.

Next, you had to make a recipe for something you truly wanted with all of your soul. No one dared say out loud that someone didn't want their wish badly enough if their recipe didn't work. No one would do what they did if they didn't all want it badly enough. Lastly, you needed The Guest, the innocent party who brought it all together by consuming their recipes unaware of the intent.

Chloe's dad was out finding The Guest right now. He'd waited until the last minute this year. Last year, he had found someone the day before, thinking they'd be washed and ready for dinner with plenty of time to spare. Instead, The Guest had made it a personal goal to see how badly they could act before they were asked to leave. They seemed to think the whole dinner was a misguided attempt at goodwill towards the less fortunate. Rutina was still mad about having to throw out that rug.

Everyone came early this year, as an undercurrent of anxiety zagged through the family. A slight twinge of concern that things needed to be extra correct after last year's failings. After all, they all had a lot to lose if dinner didn't go well. The economy was changing, and the family needed things to fall in their favor during the coming storm. Soon, the house was crowded and busy.

The family mingled over wine, waiting for the last dishes to finish. The few children present went to reacquaint themselves in front of the TV, oblivious to the rituals of their parents. Chloe's little brother greeted his cousins and presented his video game options for their appraisal.

Among the adults, knuckles cracking, and jumpy skittering made up the background soundtrack. Small talk chattered about, amplifying the brown noise until, at last, the front door opened. Chloe's dad, Trevor, had appeared with their guest of honor. The Guest.

"Hello." He called out. "Let's give our guest a moment to get settled before we eat, alright?" Beyond ready, Trevor's voice boomed across the room, too loud for the space. Behind him, a short, slightly overweight man stood, wearing too many layers of dirty clothing. The guest was naturally tan, with almond-shaped eyes and a broad, flat nose. His large belly just protruded out from beneath his sweatshirts. He looked nothing like the rest of the family. Most of the time, the guests didn't. Chloe wasn't sure what all went into the selection of The Guest, but she assumed no one wanted someone familiar. He waited in the doorway, eyes taking in the room of well-dressed dining partners.

"Please," Uncle Bart came to the door. "Come in, may I take your coat? Would you like a glass of wine?" He pulled on The Guest's wrist until the man entered the house.

The Guest cleared his throat several times before speaking. "Wine is alright." His voice was creaky, an old machine being restarted without lubrication.

A glass appeared; it had already been poured. The group congregated around the newcomer and moved him into the dining room. They sat him at the head of the table, and Trevor took the opposite end. The last of the dishes came out of the kitchen and were placed around the table. Rutina sat next to The Guest. On his other side sat her brother Tommy, who was large, muscular, and always frowning, even when he wasn't. The rest of the dining party found their seats quickly and began passing the dishes to allow everyone to plate up.

Tommy and Maggie's adult son and his fiancé were across from Chloe. Both were dressed in expensive clothing which made the designer instantly recognizable. Chloe tried not to side-eye them. Her wish would never be for anything so material. Regardless, there was a strict rule against morally policing anyone else's intentions.

This dinner was always a highly political matter. Each person was expected to serve themselves some of every dish, but also ensure enough was left for the rest of the participants. At the same time, most of them did not want to try every dish, but knew that for this to work, all of them needed to equally participate. Besides, they wouldn't want anyone to not eat *their* dish. Rutina served The Guest as each dish came by, not wanting him to slide anything by.

"What's your name, sir?" Tommy asked The Guest.

"Uh...Jose." The Guest said, while watching the plate before him fill with food.

"Good name, Jose." Tommy said, and spooned potato salad onto his plate, before passing the bowl.

"Does this, uh, potato salad, have raisins in it?" Jose pushed the pile around on his plate with a fork.

"Sure does." Tommy took a large bite. "It's got a little bit of everything we grow out on our farm. Potatoes, of course, corn, beans, peas, and raisins. Although we really grow grapes." He chuckled somehow, while still frowning. "It's for prosperity of the land."

Jose looked up at Trevor, watching him from across the table. Trevor nodded, and Jose looked away, then took a bite of a potato chunk.

Chloe watched Jose carefully. His hands were dirty and bruised, calloused, and cracked. She realized she couldn't remember the hands of any previous guests. Her house felt warmer, the walls safer, and a part of her wished the whole world could know how to find their own magic. Looking around the table, something was missing. Chloe sprang from the table and found the stack of unpassed napkins, making a quick loop around the table. At Jose's spot, she paused and placed an extra napkin next to the first. He murmured a "thank you," to which she lowered her head and rushed back to her seat.

When the casserole pans and serving dishes had all been passed around, and every plate was full, the tension broke, and the group began eating. Polite conversation peppered the air.

"May I have some salt?" Jose asked, looking back and forth between Rutina and Tommy. A hush fell over the party. Aunt Evelynn put her hand on her chest and gaped. Time stopped.

Chloe broke the silence, "I'm sorry, sir. We don't use salt."

"Oh," Jose's eye made a lap around the room, "OK." He continued to eat. After a few courses, he slowed down. Each time, one look from Trevor, and he would begin eating again with vigor. Sometimes, he'd smack his lips and give little moans of delight while his eyes remained stagnant.

The children wandered in and didn't bother to look at Jose. The tableau was of no consequence to them. They grabbed their salads and snacks, declined the dishes at the table, and found their way back to the television.

"So," Jose turned to Rutina, "Is this some kind of charity thing you folks do? Bring someone in off the streets and feed them, give them money, and send them off? Like a church thing?"

Rutina smiled, a picture of grace. "Kind of," she said with a delicate laugh. "Something like that." She looked into Jose's eyes with the warm love of a mother. "It's important to us that we do this every year, to appreciate all that we have, and hope to continue to be so blessed. We hope that you can share in the blessing, too."

Jose nodded and continued to eat.

Soon, the meal was over, and Chloe jumped up to clear everyone's dishes. Her hands shook, and it made the dishes clink.

Rutina stood and placed a hand on Jose's shoulder. "Won't you come with me, sir? I'd like to offer you a place to wash and rest before you go."

Jose looked to Trevor, who nodded again and got up from his chair to follow them. She walked him down the hall, stopping at one of several closed, unmarked doors. "Here is the bathroom. You'll find everything you need in there to get cleaned up. If you hand me your clothes, I'll get them washed and dried for you before you go. There's a robe in there for you to wear until I'm finished."

Trevor appeared behind them, making Jose jump. "Hey man," Jose began, "you said I just have to eat your family's weird food and I would get my money. You didn't say anything about a shower."

Trevor smiled wide. "I apologize, my friend. Please, go wash up. I promise you'll receive the money before you go." Jose narrowed his eyes and rocked in place. Trever let his face relax. "I'll even throw in another fifty dollars for the confusion."

Jose looked back and forth between the smiling couple. "Alright," the word came out gravelly, the temptation to respond differently clear in the sound. He turned the knob to the bathroom and let the door swing open. Rutina reached over his shoulder and flicked on the light. The bathroom was completely normal, in that older way of country chic. Pastel farm animals darted across the walls at regular intervals.

Repeating images of the same rooster, cow, and pig in different poses. A ceramic soap dispenser on the counter was pressed with the words, "Home Is Where the Heart Is." He stepped inside and turned around to look at Trevor and Rutina, both smiling, eyes glinting with a look close to doting. Trevor reached out and pulled the door closed.

Back in the dining room, the guests continued to empty wine bottles as they waited. Trevor reappeared and let the party know that their guest was washing up now. A collective cheer sounded.

"How long do you think we'll have to wait?" Tommy's wife, Maggie, asked, as she clenched the stem of her wine glass with both hands.

"Dear." Tommy patted her on the knee. "You know we need to wait for the food to digest. It's the same thing every year."

"I know," Maggie looked down, then rocked back and forth a little in her seat. "I know."

Each year on the farm had been more prosperous since the last, once they had perfected their recipe. Every time, it didn't seem like things could get any better, yet they did. Meanwhile, some of their neighbors had lost everything to the wildfires.

Rutina came down the hall a moment later and handed Chloe the pile of Jose's clothes. She wrinkled her nose and took the pile away, through the kitchen.

Trevor put on some music and Uncle Bart jumped from his seat, "Now it's a party!"

The adults began silly dancing to the music, exaggerating their movements and making each other laugh. More wine was opened, and a game of charades began. A half-hour passed, and the only person watching the time was Chloe, who sat, tapping her fingers and toes. A figure in a fluffy white bathrobe appeared in the entry to the dining room and a hush fell over the group.

"Hi." Jose smiled. "Can you give me back my clothes please?"

"Oh!" Rutina rushed to his side, "They're not dry yet. Let me show you where you can rest until they're done." She began pushing him back down the hall towards the other rooms while he gave muffled protests. A few seconds later, the rest of the family got up, one by one, and began to follow them.

Aunt Evelynn stopped Aunt Maggie in the hall. "Please? You know how desperate I am."

Maggie nodded and motioned her forward. Chloe was the last to join the chain.

At the last door in the hall, Rutina stopped and motioned Jose inside. He walked into the black room, feeling the wall for a light switch. "Hey," he called out, "I can't find the light."

The lights burst on, blinding him for a second. The room began to come into focus. Completely empty, concrete walls and floor, with some ropes and polyester straps hanging from a pulley. The floor funneled towards the center, ending in a large, manhole-sized drain. "What the?" Were the only words Jose got out before he was rushed and pinned to the ground. He tried to scream, but a large gag was shoved into his mouth and buckled in place behind his head. Eyes bulging, he began to thrash, hitting and kicking where he could. His limbs were soon subdued and bound. The bathrobe was pulled free from his naked body, and a harness strapped on instead. He continued to try and scream, muffled by the gag.

The ropes were pulled tight. Tommy and Trevor began winding a crank, Jose hadn't seen upon entering the room, next to the light switch he never found. His body slid along the floor, moving towards the center, towards the pulley over the drain. The ropes lifted his feet, pulled him further, and then his legs. Jose looked wildly from face to face, looking for an ally or even an explanation. Chloe was the only one who met his eyes. Her arms wrapped tightly around her chest, and she shook her head no. Silently, she mouthed the words, "I'm sorry."

His abdomen lifted from the ground with another turn of the crank and then, finally, his head. Several more turns, and he hoisted into the air, feet now just inches below the pulley wheel in the ceiling. Rutina approached him, holding her wine glass in one hand, and a butcher knife in the other. Jose tried to scream again.

Rutina turned to face her family. "Does everyone have their wine glass?"

Glasses were lifted into the air. She noticed Chloe's hands were empty and glanced at her husband. Trevor left, then reappeared with an empty glass, which he pushed into his daughter's hands. Chloe took it and held it upside down in one hand while she covered her face with the other. She'd had an idea of what was about to happen, but she'd never been allowed in the room before today. For some reason, she always thought that The Guest went willingly, honored to be partaking. Now, she didn't know where that idea had come from.

"Alright, then, let's begin." Rutina raised her glass up high. "From our hearts to his, let the dreams we wish be granted through his blood, returned to us pure and holy."

The rest of the family raised their glasses and repeated the refrain back to her. She turned to face Jose and tucked her empty glass under one arm. She steadied his head with one hand and used the knife to make a quick, deep, practiced puncture into his jugular vein. Blood poured out. Jose continued to try and scream. Rutina held her glass under the pouring stream until a couple ounces had filled it. "Quickly, everyone, while it's fresh and warm."

The family lined up and Evelynn rushed to be at the front. They filled their glasses, then drank deeply. Some savored, knowing the power of the sacrifice. Others chugged, wanting to get past it quickly. Maggie's glass sloshed across her face and dripped down the sides of her cheeks. Chloe hung back as she watched her family collect their sacrament. Each person except her had now drank their share. They turned to her, watching, and waiting. Jose's eyes had begun closing, a sleepy expression clouded him.

"Chloe." Rutina approached her daughter and gently squeezed her shoulder. "We all have to drink, or else..." She pulled Chloe over to Jose's hanging body and pushed her daughter's glass under the diminishing stream of blood. It spilled over the back of Chloe's hand, and the warmth startled her. The glass filled, and Rutina let go. Chloe stumbled back and looked down at her hands as though she'd never seen them before.

"Chloe." Her dad stepped forward, "drink, Honey."

"Yes, Chloe." Her Aunt Evelynn held her empty glass in one hand and the other placed over her womb, "please drink?"

The group spoke in chorus. "Drink, Chloe, drink."

A bead of sweat ran down Chloe's neck into her cleavage. It felt like a spider.

Chloe raised her glass.

The Cave

Cody followed his friend's footsteps into the night. His flashlight lit up the bottom of Taylor's sneakers as he walked through the woods on the mushy ground. It had stopped raining a few hours ago and was in that late night reprieve from winter precipitation. It would always let up by ten pm and stay clear until at least around two or so. Perfect timing for sneaking out after his parents went to bed and being back before his stepdad got up for work at three am sharp. Thankfully, tonight was a Saturday, and he didn't have to get up early for school tomorrow. Not that he was doing much his senior year anyhow.

The light from the flashlight being carried behind him flashed his shadow over the path at times, making it so he'd stumble, unable to see where to step. The lights were bright, large, heavy duty, and metal, way better than their phones would have been. He stumbled again.

"Dude," Cody tossed a look over his shoulder, "Keep your light aimed at the ground, OK?"

"Sorry Bro." Liam snickered.

Cody didn't know why Taylor had invited him, unless he had some good weed. Since they were all still in high school, it was hard to get the good shit. He wondered if Liam's mom was a daily toker, the kind who wouldn't notice the occasional nugget going missing.

Cody had never been this far out in the woods before. The guys had told him they'd found a sweet new smoking spot. They always enjoyed finding a spot in the woods where they could smoke or drink without being bothered. Plus, it was fun when they brought girls out with them. They could always act like they heard a bear or something, and the girls would snuggle in tight for protection. The usual spots had seen a lot of action since they started going. But this wasn't anywhere near those places. Cody wasn't even sure where they were. They'd been walking for so long. At least 25 minutes now. The light behind him flared up again. Cody tripped over a tree root and went face first into the soft dirt that blanketed the forest floor.

"What the fuck!" Cody pushed himself up into a sitting position. Both of his travel companions swung their lights into his face, blinding him.

Taylor offered his hand. "What happened?"

"Sorry man." The corners of Liam's mouth curled. He was trying to suppress a smile. That motherfucker.

"Get the lights out of my face." Cody grabbed Taylor's arm with one hand and wiped his cheeks off with the other. He tossed Liam an angry look. They resumed their trek.

A few minutes later, they rounded a bend and confronted a steep cliff face that lifted straight out of the ground. It was as though a giant had dropped a skyscraper there. A clear path ran alongside the stone wall. They turned left and kept walking. Up ahead, Taylor had stopped and was facing the stone, shining his light on it, but instead of lighting up, the beam seemed to disappear into the air. Cody came up next to him and found he was facing the opening to a cave.

"Woah," Cody said and lifted his flashlight to look inside, but nothing illuminated. It must be deep.

Liam joined them and looked over to Taylor, "you pussies ready?"

Taylor's breathing had sped up over the last few seconds since they arrived. Cody wasn't aware of his friend having claustrophobia, this was new to him. He'd known the guy since kindergarten, but that didn't mean there weren't secrets. It's not like you can know everything about a person. Even your best friend. He smacked Taylor on the shoulder, "hey man, it's cool. We don't have to go in. We can just sit out here and smoke."

Taylor wouldn't turn to look at him and continued staring into the blackness of the cave, waiting for something that never appeared. He took a couple of quick, deep breaths and stomped into the cave.

Liam burst out laughing. He motioned his arm in a wide arc, waving the way forward. "After you, my good sir." Cody rolled his eyes and took a step inside the cave.

Sweeping his light from side to side, nothing but a rocky floor lit up. The cave was wide, much larger than they would have guessed. He made sure to be careful as he stepped; the rocks were slick. He felt something push into his spine. "Hurry up man, don't want to be late." Liam sang it in a taunting way.

"Fuck off, dude, I'm being careful. If you shove me again, I'm gonna deck you."

"Alright, alright." Liam said chuckled again.

A few more steps in and his light found Taylor. He was standing in front of a ledge where the rocks formed a small stage. Liam moved around Cody and jumped up onto the flat rocks. "Nice Bro, let's light up."

Cody took a few more small steps and stopped next to Taylor. His friend continued to take shallow, rapid breaths, hyping himself up. On the ledge, Liam had sat down and loaded a glass pipe. "Relax already. Have a fucking hit." He flicked his lighter and took a deep inhale off the pipe. Liam closed his eyes and let the smoke escape in a long, slow stream from his mouth, then held out the pipe to the other boys. Taylor lifted his flashlight high and, taking a quick step forward, brought it down hard upon Liam's head.

Cody screamed, and Liam crumpled to the ground. Taylor leaned over Liam's body and continued to beat at his head with the flashlight, silent. The only sounds were the wet, breaking thump each time the metal light hit, interrupted by Cody's screaming. After a dozen whacks, Taylor stumbled backwards into the cave wall and slid to the ground. Cody was still screaming. He thought to check on Liam, but his face was a bloody, unrecognizable mess. His breath ran out, making him cough, and he yelled, "WHAT THE FUCK, TAYLOR! WHY THE FUCK DID YOU DO THAT?"

Taylor sat on the ground, staring out into the darkness. "I'm sorry," he mumbled. Blood on the lens of the flashlight cast a red glow around them. "I'm sorry."

Cody screamed again and followed it with screaming "FUCK" at the top of his lungs. He took a step towards Taylor and stopped himself. "Why, man, why did you do it? What the fuck."

"I had to." Taylor looked up at his friend for the first time. "I had to stop him."

"What?" Cody realized he had tears streaming from his eyes and ran his sleeve across his cheek. "Stop him, what the fuck are you talking about, man? We were just smoking a bowl."

"No, I just, just look, okay?" Taylor got up and walked back over to Liam's unmoving body. He lifted the side of the blood covered jacket and shined the red light on the contents. Inside there was a small roll of duct tape, some zip ties, two large hunting knives, and a semiautomatic pistol.

"What? What? What the fuck is going on? Oh my god. We need to get out of here. Taylor, what the fuck did you do?"

"He was gonna kill you, man!" Taylor now raised his voice to match Cody's. "He was gonna fucking kill you!"

"What?"

"He wanted to bring you out here and kill you. Said he needed a sacrifice and if I helped him, we were going to be rich."

Cody let out a strangled noise and ran his hands through his hair. "What?"

"I thought he was off his fucking rocker, or joking or something, but I listened to him. And he was serious, Cody, he was fucking serious."

"Sacrifice?"

"If it wasn't you, it was going to be someone else. And if it wasn't me that helped him, then that was going to be someone else, too. I had to stop him."

"Oh my god, Taylor, God Taylor, fuck, he was probably kidding man. Oh my god."

Taylor lifted the edge of the jacket higher, making Liam's body turn forward, facing Cody. "Will you fucking look? Look at this shit! Does this look like he was fucking joking?"

Cody glanced up, took in the weapons again, and looked away. "Fuck. I think I'm going to be sick."

"I had to, Cody, I had to."

"Okay, okay, I get it, I guess. No, I don't get it. Why didn't you just tell someone?"

"I told you, if it wasn't you or me, it would be someone else. If I told anyone, he would have just told them he was kidding. Who the fuck believes in human sacrifices? No one, it's ridiculous. No one would think he was serious. And then he'd just do it to someone else."

"Fuck. Okay, well, why didn't you tell me?"

"Would you have believed me? Helped?"

"I don't know, I don't know. Fuck."

Cody crouched down and held his face in his hands. He couldn't stop crying. He didn't care, and he knew Taylor wouldn't care either. They'd seen each other cry over the years, when a dog died, when a girl left, when Cody's real dad left. When Taylor's mom died. This was the least of his worries.

Taylor came over and placed his hand on Cody's shoulder. "I need you to help me hide the body."

"Fuck," Cody's voice was hoarse, and it came out almost a whisper. He nodded his head. "Just gimme a sec." He couldn't see it, but he knew Taylor was nodding his head back. They held this pose for a moment, Cody crouching on the ground, Taylor standing next to him, still touching his shoulder, light aimed on Liam's torso.

Taylor paused and cocked his head to the side. "Cody, do you hear that?"

Cody looked up and then turned his head away when he realized he was looking at Liam's bashed in face. He shut his eyes and listened. He could hear it. Rustling.

A sound like rushing water, but not. The sound of

thousands, no, millions of tiny legs rushing in the same direction. It was coming from deeper into the cave. Cody stood up. They both lifted their lights at the same time into the darkness. At first, nothing but the darkness greeted them back. They each took a step backwards. The first one appeared.

A small millipede, hard to see in the light, came scurrying over a rock from deeper within the cave. It had a bright red stripe running down its otherwise black, glossy body. It raised the front half of its body and pointed its head in their direction. The boys took another step back. Another appeared. A wave of small red lines flowed over the rocks twenty feet away from them. In sync, they both began to run.

The tsunami of millipedes came crashing around them from either side while they ran for the entrance. In seconds, the surrounding millipedes blocked off the way, and the insects piled into a mound directly in their path. Cody and Taylor looked and each other, both panicked and unsure what to do. The pile of insects grew, and a second pile appeared next to the first. Both lifted higher until several feet off the ground and joined as an arch. The arch kept growing taller until a large mass formed at the apex of the towers, and then a head shaped mound took shape on top . The body of the creature was in constant motion, crawling with insects as they wriggled around while holding the shape of a giant man-thing in front of them. Arms began extending out of the shoulders and ended in fat, thick fingers of skittering bugs.

It glided forward one step. The legs didn't detach from the ground, never breaking the chain of moving insects, yet moving one at a time as though shifting its weight from one leg to the other. Taylor screamed. They turned to look behind them. The millipedes were everywhere.

Liam's body was now an unrecognizable giant lump

covered with the insects. Taylor screamed again.

"No!" Taylor grabbed Cody's arm. "It's what he said. IT'S WHAT HE SAID."

A millipede fell from the air and landed on Taylor's face. He yelped and took off towards the entrance, trying to dodge the moving figure as it advanced. Millipedes swarmed up on either side of him and covered his body. He disappeared behind the human-like figure still gliding forward. Cody could hear Taylor still screaming, coming from the darkness behind it.

It approached Cody and stopped. Cody could not see any distinguishing features that would indicate eyes or a mouth, yet it seemed to regard him, evaluating. It nodded its head once, an acknowledgment, and then glided past. Cody swiveled to watch.

The figure descended on the mound that once was Liam. It collapsed over the body, tripling the size of the pile. The noise of scurrying intensified, and it shook him like the world was screaming into his ears. The pile began shrinking. It grew smaller and smaller, and the legions of millipedes receded back into the depths of the cave.

Cody was a statue, terrified to shift his weight. The millipedes went, a wave crashing on rewind. They uncovered where Liam should have been. Nothing remained. The sound of the rushing continued for a while after the last insect disappeared. It diminished until silence resumed. He couldn't believe how quiet the cave was. Not a sound from the outside infiltrated the space. Remembering Taylor, he whipped around, stiff from having held still for so long. He could see no sign of his friend in between him and the front of the cave. "Taylor?" He called into the darkness.

The flight response kicked in. He rushed for the opening. He found himself able to navigate the slick rocks with ease now. Cody burst into the moonlight and stopped. "Taylor?" he yelled louder. No response. A breeze tickled his neck, a breeze coming from inside the cave. He turned and ran.

Halfway back to the car. His phone rang. The noise made him scream and stumble, but not fall. It was his mom. He answered it, slowing from a sprint to a jog. "Mom?" The word came out choked, the sound of grief and fear and terror all rolled into a single prayer for comfort.

"Cody?" His mom screamed his name, sounding elated. "Cody, where are you? Honey, we won the lottery! We won! We won!"

"What?" Cody wanted to stop jogging, but fear drove him forward. "Mom, are you serious?"

"Yes! I couldn't sleep and got up to find my phone and found an old lotto ticket in my purse. I checked it and we won. We're millionaires, baby!" She screamed an incoherent "woohoo," into the phone. "Where are you? Get home! We need to plan! We need to celebrate!"

"I'm coming, Mom?"

"Yes Cody? Oh my god, I'm so excited, get home!"

"Mom…" He wanted to tell her about Taylor, about Liam and the bugs, but the words wouldn't come. The thought slapped him. No one would believe him. "Mom, I'll be there soon. I love you."

"I love you, Cody! Millionaires!" She yelled "woohoo," into the phone again and hung up.

He reached the car and made it home in record time, silent tears dripping down his cheeks for the entire drive.

He never wanted for anything again. They'd won enough money to do everything they'd ever wanted. He had no reason to go to college, but did anyway, wanting reasons to get far away from where he'd grown up. Taylor's dad had called the police the next day. Liam's parents the day after. A search was done, and it was decided that the two boys had run away together. They questioned Cody briefly and left him alone after that. Everyone knew how upsetting it must have been to lose his best friend this way. By him running off with someone and never thinking of inviting you. People assumed they must have had a falling out beforehand that Cody didn't want to talk about.

After spending a decade bouncing around various colleges, and then grad schools, Cody accepted a last degree and decided to travel the world. He stayed in the nicest hotels and napped on private beaches. He tried out a few religions, and many drugs. Anything to help him sleep. He found out he could exhaust himself to the point of being able to pass out if he tried hard enough and became an extreme sports enthusiast. Staying asleep was the problem, because then the nightmares would come back. When his normal dreams would fade to black and all he would hear is the sound of millions of insect legs rushing towards him, covering his body, and when he went to scream, filling his mouth, skittering, wriggling.

The Box

"Essie, hurry up, get in the box!"

"No Mom! This is stupid. We don't even know if bombs are actually coming!"

"Essie, we heard it on the news, for Pete's sake! We're running out of time. Come here and get in the Goddamn box!"

"No Mom! No!"

The sirens began their undulating wail. Normally reserved for tornadoes, the local government didn't know what else to use to inform anyone who hadn't been following the conflict. Her little brother began to sob. He wails chorused in tune with the sirens.

Her dad shouted from the floor, "Fuck! Essie, get in the fucking box! We're running out of time!"

The family had been planning. Prepping. They'd been watching their feeds, trying to decide if what they'd heard for the last couple years was an exaggeration or truth. To be safe, they'd started stockpiling: dry goods, bottled water, ammo, and first aid supplies. Their biggest purchase before the box was a fireproof safe to hold the important things. The irreplaceable things, things like: IDs, court records, jewelry, that weird family heirloom Essie had never liked. It was what gave them the idea.

When the news channels started discussing the possibility of nukes, Essie's Mom had joked about wishing they could all fit in the safe to hide. Jokes turned into a giggling attempt to fit the kids inside. Essie curled up on the floor with her brother awkwardly balanced on her shoulders. The attempt was both scary and exciting for them at the time. Kind of like getting locked in the trunk for a minute after unloading groceries. All in good fun.

Dad had begun sincerely discussing how to build such a thing with his father and brother, who also lived with them in the large country house. None of them were engineers or worked in construction, but they figured, how difficult could a box be? They considered materials, it would need to be fireproof, more like bomb proof really. What thickness of stainless steel to get? How well insulated. It needed to be large enough to fit the whole family. They didn't keep any pets, only chickens for the eggs and a pig to harvest for meat once a year. They figured the family only needed to be locked inside for the initial blast, and the house could be sealed for the fallout or drift that came after.

It would need a handle that could be locked from the inside, so scavengers couldn't try to force their way in. Grampa kept calling them carpetbaggers and pirates. No telling what someone might do in the face of the apocalypse.

The box would need some cushioning so it wouldn't be too uncomfortable. The men had figured it would be easier to lie down for a few hours, rather than stand or squat. After evaluating the placement for a while, the plan came together. The floorboards in the back room were ripped up. The house hadn't been built with a proper basement, just three feet of empty space between the floor and the dirt. The whole space was surrounded by concrete foundation walls which traced the house's footprint.

There, they built the box. Layers of sheet metal. Insulation. Steel and aluminum. More insulation. The walls had ended up about eight inches thick on all sides. It rose out of the center of the ripped-up floor like some kind of giant metal stage when the lid was down. They soldered it together layer by layer. Damn thing took six months to finish. Then of course, nothing happened. Essie was afraid someone would come over and see it, and then she'd have to explain how crazy her family was.

A year went by, and it seemed like the conflict was deescalating. Until, it wasn't. Until a peace talk had gone horribly wrong. Until it was discovered by a drone that actions had been taken, and promises had been broken. Until a statement was made publicly in anger. A statement that couldn't be taken back. Especially not by an egomaniac.

If they heard right away, people had gotten a few hours' notice that things had gone wrong. The most likely landing sites were identified, and the world panicked. The adults in the family felt prepared.

The box had been lined with thin mats and blankets. Adult diapers had been purchased and were now fitted under sweatpants. Cans of oxygen were tucked against the sides. High-calorie protein bars and bottles of water stashed. Each family member had their own flashlight and extra batteries, with instructions to use them as little as possible. Essie's little brother thought it was a great adventure at first. The men spoke in earnest of rebuilding after the fall, and eyed Essie when they thought she wasn't looking. They seemed to think that healthy young women would be in high demand.

Everyone felt proud of their ingenuity. Everyone; except Essie. She hated the box. She thought her parents were paranoid losers. No one online, where she hung out, suggested stuffing their family in a giant metal box to survive a nuke. Her mom had done some of the things Essie had read about when the notice came. That woman had run around like mad, filling every pot and tub in the house with water. Sealing cracks with duct tape, turning off the air. She'd covered every window, and now not a spec of daylight entered the house at three pm in the afternoon. And the worst part of this all? The box stunk.

Essie hated the way it smelled and the idea of being trapped in there for hours, maybe days, with the stench of her unwashed family? It was just too much. Too much.

Now, her mom was tugging on her arm, trying to pull her in.

Essie's dad, her grampa, uncle, and little brother were all safely tucked inside already. The box was only big enough for the family to lay side by side, shoulders touching. There was enough clearance for them to roll over each other awkwardly if needed. The lid was hinged with a hydraulic lift on the far side. All that needed to be done was for her and her mom to climb in and pull the handle down. Her brother lay clutching his favorite stuffed animal under one arm and his tablet in the other. His favorite cartoons were already downloaded and playing silently on a screen that might never be charged again.

"Essie, GET IN THE FUCKING BOX!" Her mom was

screaming now. Echoed by shouts from the men already tucked inside.

Her mom had managed to wrench her to the edge. Essie yanked back against her. The older woman now stood inside the box, pulling with all her might. The sirens sounded louder somehow.

The older woman yanked again, pulling Essie partially over the edge. She jammed her feet against the side, pulling backward until it felt like her wrists would break. Her mom reached up with one hand to grab the handle and began to pull it closed. "Get in, Essie, get in!"

Essie jumped up and kicked a leg out, slamming it with a *thwump* into her mother's side. The older woman stumbled back, letting go of Essie's arm; and falling on top of her family. Yelps erupted from the group, and she heard the high-pitched shriek of her brother beginning to cry.

With one hand, Essie reached up for the handle and swung it down as hard as she could, falling backward in the process. She collapsed onto the wood floor, knocking the wind out of herself. The hydraulics worked. The motion helped the lid glide easily into place. She lay, gasping for breath, staring at the sealed box. The sirens continued. A different high-pitched noise started from somewhere outside the house.

Essie got up and stumbled, in pain from her fall. Surprised, she realized that the inside handle of the box was still tightly within her grip. She dropped it to the floor and ran for the nearest cupboard.

The house shook, and then, shattered.

The family inside the box felt the boom, and they were fine. They heard the distant cacophony and her uncle giggled hysterically. The house was coming down around them. Essie's mom cried in silence, broken at the loss of her only daughter, her first child, half of her heart.

The noises soon stopped. The men gave humble cheers at their success.

"How long should we stay?" Asked the uncle, his tone unhinged.

Essie's dad responded, "We have our diapers on. We don't know how bad the fallout is. We should stay until we've used up all the supplies, or at least the oxygen."

Silence then, while the family thought it over. Essie's Little Brother whimpered.

"But how," The mother's words were ragged through her tears. "How are we going to get out?"

Her husband's words tumbled out; he'd been expecting the question. "The hydraulic lift should be able to work as long as the debris on top isn't too bad. We may have to push together to help it up."

"No," Essie's mom sniffled and turned on the small flashlight she'd pulled from her pocket. "I mean, how. How are we going to get out?"

The rest of the family turned and lifted themselves up on their elbows to see what she illuminated. The space where the door handle should have been, a circle of spotlight around it. No part of the handle remained, just a mostly flat surface where the handle had broken off cleanly.

Essie's Brother reached up with one finger and rubbed it along the space where the handle used to be. "It's gone," he said.

I Remember You

Kyle clutched the arms of the easy chair. His teenage son slouched against the wall in front of him, dressed as he normally would, except for three things that stood out as being distinctly wrong. Leo now sported hair long enough to put into a ponytail, painted his nails electric green, and, for the first time that Kyle had ever seen, had his eyes rimmed with mascara.

It was Sunday morning, and Leo had just gotten back from staying the night at a friend's house. Kyle stood up, having decided.

"Get your coat. We're going to church." Kyle's tone was authoritarian, granite in its firmness.

Leo shrugged and pulled his hoody on.

After service, Kyle told his son to wait in the pew while he went to speak to the preacher. She was tall and kind looking. A bit too plain for his taste, but, whatever, you didn't need to be hot to preach the word of the lord. People were milling around her, making small talk before heading next door for coffee cake. He got close to her and kept his voice to a whisper. "Preacher Sally, Could I bother you for a sec?"

She raised her eyebrows and motioned towards her office. After entering the small room, Kyle turned and closed the door, listening for the click before turning to face her.

"Preacher, I think I have a problem."

She sat on the edge of her desk, shoulders back, head high. "What can I help you with, Kyle?"

"It's Leo. Something's not right with him. He's changed. I think he's under the influence of something."

"You think he's doing drugs?"

"No!" Kyle startled himself with the quickness of his response and ran his hands through his hair. "No, I think, something's got a hold of him, making him act funny."

The preacher sat, waiting for Kyle to continue. After a pause, she asked, "Has he fallen in with a bad crowd?"

"No, no, not like that. He's acting weird. Not like himself. He's doing weird stuff. He painted his nails, for Pete's sake."

"Oh, I see." She let out a long sigh, understanding crossing her features. "Kyle, sometimes kids don't turn out the way we planned them to. They might not be who we want them to be, or love who we want them to love, but in the end, it's all part of God's plan. It's important we learn to accept our children for who they are."

Kyle lunged forward. "He's not gay! All right? There's something wrong with him." He stopped and registered the fearful expression on the preacher's face. "Look." Kyle shut his eyes and forced the anger from his voice. "Do you believe in possession, like, demon possession? Have you ever seen that happen?"

"Kyle, you're worrying me. Why would you ask such a thing?"

He took a deep breath and dropped his shoulders. "Will you, just, spend some time with him? Talk to him? Tell me what you think?"

She stood and nodded. "That's a good idea. Why don't you send him in?"

Kyle made an audible "phew" noise and left the room. Leo entered a minute later, and Kyle smiled at both of them before shutting the door behind him.

After twenty minutes of waiting, Leo and Sally exited smiling, still talking. Kyle approached, scuffing his feet with each step. "Hey," he said, stopping several feet back from the pair.

Leo looked up at his dad and then at the preacher, words unspoken in his eyes. The preacher squeezed the teenager's shoulder and leaned over to whisper in his ear. Kyle just caught the words, "Remember, you can call me anytime."

Leo nodded and walked past his dad without acknowledging him. Kyle mouthed the words "thank you" to the preacher, and raised his eyebrows. They waited until Leo had left the church before speaking.

"Everything seems fine to me Kyle, I think he's just going through normal teenage stuff. But, come back anytime if something happens, okay?"

Kyle mumbled another "thank you" and left, fist clenched, nails digging into his palms as he walked.

In the truck on the way home, Kyle fidgeted in the silence, jangling his keychain. He soon broke. "How'd your talk with the preacher go?"

"Fine."

"Just fine?"

"Yeah."

"Well, uh, what did you two talk about?"

Leo remained silent. Kyle turned to glance at his son and found the teen leaning towards him, staring. Kyle jumped, and the truck veered in its lane. "What the heck Leo, why are you looking at me like that?"

The voice came. Not Leo's, but the voice Leo spoke in only to him. Higher pitched and effeminate, a lilting, whimsical tone edged with playfulness. "You think you really did something there, don't you?"

Kyle gripped the steering wheel harder, resisting the urge he always got to slap his son when he sounded like this.

"Leo, I've told you, I'm not going to respond when you speak to me like that."

His son continued in the same tone. "Come on, Kyle, do you really think I'm possessed?" Do you really believe I have a demon," the teenager paused and began rubbing himself passionately, "all up in this?"

Kyle turned into their driveway. "I said knock it off, Leo."

"Which one is it, daddy? Azaphet? Beelzebub? Lucifer herself? Name me and perhaps I'll leave."

Thunder cracked outside from the early winter storm moving in. Today would be spent watching T.V. and wondering where the hell he went wrong as a parent. Kyle opened his door. "Better get inside. Your mom will want help prepping dinner. Grammie and Papaw are coming over tonight."

He slammed the door and walked towards the house, leaving his teenage son still caressing himself in the car.

Inside, Kyle stopped to kiss his wife, Darla, on the cheek before she waved him away. She looked up from the biscuit dough she was cutting. "Is Leo coming in soon? I want him to help clean the shrimp."

Kyle grimaced. "I don't know Darl; he's being weird again."

She laughed and shook her head. Kyle left to go put on the game. She'd never seen how their son gets. No one did, besides him. The T.V. did little to distract him. He hoped that this was some long prank or weird teenage phase, but the way Leo spoke to him, the energy in his eyes, made Kyle's skin crawl.

The front door opened, closed, and Kyle realized there was someone standing behind him. He swiveled the big recliner to see Leo, standing statue still. His head leaned at an unnatural angle, and his mouth hung open, slack, and eyes rolled inwards; only showing the whites.

Darla yelled from the kitchen. "Leo? Hun? I need you to come help me clean the shrimp."

Leo's limp mouth clamped shut, reopened, and then his lips and tongue jumped around in a series of erratic motions, as though he'd forgotten how to speak. "Coming mom." He said in his normal voice. As soon as the words finished, his mouth dropped back open.

Kyle cleared his throat and leaned back in his chair. "You better go help your mom, Leo."

Leo took several sudden, brief steps up to Kyle and stopped inches away from where he sat. Leo's face still tilted up and away at the same weird angle. The game droned on in the background while neither one moved.

Leo's head slowly rolled forward and down until facing Kyle, although his eyes were still rotated back into his head. He took slow, heavy breaths, as though laboring under an immense load. A string of drool slipped out of his mouth and stretched until it broke, landing in a small puddle on Kyle's knee.

His mouth began jumping around again, searching for

memories of how to speak. "I was only fourteen," were the words that rose to the surface.

Kyle jumped to his feet; fists clenched, now standing face to face with his son. "You ARE only fourteen Leo. Now go help your mother!"

Leo's eyes flew into focus, and he blinked several times. "Okay," he said and shrugged, before running out of the room.

Kyle huffed, catching his breath, heart hammering in his chest. He wasn't a weirdo, Darla wasn't a weirdo, how could he have had such a weird fucking kid?

The doorbell rang. His parents were early. Darla was going to be annoyed as hell. Kyle almost ran for the door.

The rest of the evening passed without event, and Kyle felt the most normal he'd felt in weeks since Leo first began this behavior. Kyle wondered if a change of pace would be what Leo needed. Maybe he should go stay with his grandparents for a while, or maybe one of those camps for troubled kids. Maybe a Catholic boarding school. Wouldn't that make his Methodist grandmother have a stroke. Kyle snorted at the idea, and looked up to see the whole family staring at him.

"Something funny?" Kyle's mother asked.

"Ah, no, just remembering something I saw on the internet today."

"Oh, the internet!" his mother rolled her eyes. "Here I thought I'd have to be worried about my grandson spending all his free time on the internet. Instead, I find Leo being a perfect gentleman and my son being the one who can't put his phone down."

"Sorry mom." Kyle could feel the heat in his cheeks. Across the table, he could see Leo hiding his smirk. He swallowed the urge to yell and instead dug into his food, taking the repressed emotions out on his stomach.

That night, after his parents left, Kyle tried to relax with a beer while watching the news. Darla looked up from her book on the couch and told him, "Leo's been in the shower for a while now. Mind going to check on him?"

Kyle frowned and made a mental note to buy extra lotion and tissues for the hallway bathroom. He waited until the commercial break and thundered up the stairs, trying to be as loud as possible. At the door, a strange noise reached his ears, a muttering mixed with crying, coming from inside the bathroom.

"Leo?" Kyle pounded on the door. "You okay?"

Incoherent noises radiated from the other side. It sounded like two people arguing and all Kyle could hear at the end was a whimpering "no, no, no."

Kyle threw open the door.

Leo sat on the floor, naked, arms wrapped around himself in a hug, head down. The shower was running full blast with the curtain open wide, dripping water everywhere.

"Leo, what the fuck?" Kyle darted inside and turned off the water. The mumbling became clearer.

In a pitiful, child-like voice, Leo was repeating, "don't tell him, don't tell him, he'll do it again. No, no, no."

Kyle saw his son was rocking back and forth. "Kiddo, what are you doing?"

Leo's head popped up and looked at his father's face. His hands let go of his skinny body and reached up until wrapped around his own neck. Leo began to strangle himself.

His hands wrapped tighter and tighter, until the boy was choking, his face turning red. Eyes locked on his father's, Leo gasped the word "help."

"Leo!" Kyle yelled and threw himself onto his son. Leo thrashed and struggled as Kyle tried to pry his hands away from his throat.

Darla appeared in the background and yelled, "what is going on in here?"

Leo went slack. Kyle dropped his son's wrists and backed away. Leo curled up into a ball on the floor.

Darla stood with her hands on her hips. "What the heck were you two doing?"

"Dad attacked me." Leo said in a shuddering voice and let out a wailing cry.

"Kyle!" Darla yelled and inserted herself between the two.

"He was choking himself!" Kyle scrambled to his feet. "He was trying to strangle himself like a Goddamn crazy person!"

Leo whimpered and snuggled into his mother's legs.

Darla's face hardened. "Kyle, get out."

Kyle stormed from the bathroom. He slept on the couch that night.

In the morning, he got up early and put the coffee on. When it was ready, he poured it into a travel mug, sweetened it with creamer and carried it upstairs, careful not to spill a drop. Their bedroom door was cracked. He stopped before going in. "Darla? You up? I made coffee, babe. We need to talk about Leo."

A muffled "hmm?" came from beyond the door. Kyle pushed the door open with his shoulder, letting the hall light illuminate the room.

In their queen-sized bed, Darla lay asleep, curled up and facing away from him. Sitting up next to her, bare chested, was Leo, smirking.

Leo laughed in the same distorted voice from the truck, and asked, "What is it about Leo that we should talk about? Hmm?"

Kyle's mouth dried up. "Get out." He rasped. "Get the fuck out of here."

Leo laughed again. "Careful, don't want to wake

mommy." He pulled back the covers and stood up, still naked from the night before. He sauntered over to Kyle, who stepped back to let him through. Leo stopped and smirked again at his father before walking away to his own room, hips swaying with each step.

Kyle started following before he knew what he was doing. He came into the teenager's bedroom behind his son and pushed the door shut. Leo whirled and pressed his body against his father's, wrapping his arms around the large man and tipped his head up. Kyle froze.

Leo made a purring noise and said, "I think this has gone on long enough, don't you?"

"What the fuck did you do to your mother, you little shit?"

Leo threw his head back and laughed. He dropped his arms and walked over to his bed, rolling onto his side, and propping his head up on one hand. "Oh, daddy Kyle, do you still not get it? Do you not remember me? I remember you."

Kyle paused. He was still holding the hot coffee and considered throwing it onto his child. Instead, he set it down on the nearby dresser and sighed.

"Okay Leo, I'll play. Who are you?"

Leo laughed again, through the distorted voice. "I guess if it's not obvious yet, will this help you remember?" Leo flopped onto his back and spread his legs wide, then began thrusting his hips up and down. In an even higher-pitched voice he said, "please stop, mister stop, you're hurting me. Stop, please stop!"

Leo ceased thrusting and threw his hands to his throat, clawing at something that wasn't there. "No, please, stop, no." He pretended to lose consciousness and fell limp against his mattress.

Kyle's face was bright red. He yanked the door open so hard it cracked, and he ran out, back down the hall, shaking the entire way. Throughout the house, he heard Leo's squealing laughter ringing in his ears.

He found his keys, got in his truck, and left. Not sure where else to go, he drove to work early at the factory and took a cold shower in the locker room.

That day he was so distracted, he almost smashed his hand inside the box former, and nearly backed over someone while driving the forklift. His boss wrote him up and told him to go home early. During his drive, Kyle noticed the local sports bar had opened for lunch. He turned in.

After a plate of fried food that he poked at, and five sipped beers, he knew he had to go home. Staying any later would require an explanation for Darla, and he wasn't sure he was ready for that.

Darla was plating the table when he walked in. Leo was already seated, face washed, in clean clothes. Kyle squared his shoulders and sat down across from his son.

"Oh shucks." Darla said from the kitchen. She stuck her head around the corner to where she could see them. "I spilled sauce all over myself. I'm just gonna run upstairs real quick and change. All right?"

She looked back and forth between the two of them. "You two gonna be okay alone for a few minutes?"

Father and son both smiled and reassured her things would be fine.

"That's my boys." She returned the smile and disappeared.

Both Leo and Kyle waited until they could hear that her footsteps were far enough away.

"All right." Kyle's hands were curled into fists, that he forced to relax. "What is it you want? Money?"

"What am I supposed to do with money, Kyle? I'm dead."

"I could send it to your family?"

"They were the assholes who sold me in the first place,

Kyle." Leo and the entity inside him folded his arms and jutted his chin out.

Kyle groaned. "What then? What will it take to make you go away?"

"Oh, you piece of shit." Leo laughed, the high-pitched, unnatural laugh, stopped abruptly and leaned forward. "You think you can go to another country, rape and murder a teenage girl? Drop her in a trash pile, and have no consequences?"

Kyle swallowed and blinked several times.

His son continued. "All I want is my life back, but I don't get to have that, do I? There is no way I ever get to be me in my body, ever, ever again. So here's the deal, Anytime I want to be alive, I'm going to borrow Leo here, as long as he lets me. And if I'm ever ready to let go, I'll leave. And there's not a fucking thing you can do about it."

Kyle's eyebrows skyrocketed. He had to clear his throat several times before speaking. "He lets you?"

"You heard me right. I told Leo everything that happened to me. I just didn't tell him who. He's more than happy to let me live again in him, and you will be, too. If you don't want him to find out."

Darla's voice rang out, "who's ready for dinner?" and she breezed into the room. "Looks like you two are getting along again, ready to eat?"

Kyle's throat burned and the room dimmed. He started coughing, and coughing, and couldn't catch his breath. He doubled over, hacking, unable to breathe. Darla ran to get him water. It took several sips and a choking lungful of air to calm down. He settled himself and sat upright again.

Across the table, his son looked at him with genuine concern. In his completely normal voice he asked, "are you okay, Dad?"

Burnout

The day Missy's soul finally broke, the disfigured child had lain on the floor moaning for hours. It did that a lot. She'd been staring at it groping around on the kitchen linoleum, the smell of its shit filled diaper permeated the air.

Six years ago, Missy had barely discovered she was pregnant when she'd gone into labor. For months she figured she'd just been getting fatter. Heartburn was typical for her, as were abnormal periods. There'd been no prenatal care. No developmental ultrasounds. Severe abdominal pain she'd been sure was appendicitis or even gallstones had ended in a shocking emergency department visit. A nurse had given her the news; she was roughly twenty-eight weeks pregnant, and now in labor.

The entire experience had slipped by in a numb blur. The child was blind, deaf, and would probably never walk, or speak, learn how to use a toilet, or wash itself. There was a high likelihood it would die in infanthood. A multitude of stacked syndromes. They'd won the worst kind of lottery. Despite all that, they sent mother and baby home two months later with promised visits from a social worker. Alone, of course, her boyfriend had bailed the day after the doctors had given them the prognosis for the child.

Missy hadn't even wanted to name her. a young nurse's aide had suggested "Emily" and Missy had nodded, allowing the name to be written on the birth certificate. It's not that Missy had anything against naming the baby, she was simply too numb to feel any emotional pull towards a name. Why, she wondered, was she required to name something she hadn't known was coming, and now would never even get to know.

Despite what the doctors said, the baby thrived. It wasn't so bad when it was small, compact, easy to control. Things had gotten harder when the child had grown in size and became stronger. Despite what all the paperwork said, Missy couldn't bring herself to call the child Emily. It couldn't hear her anyhow. There was nothing about the thing that showed humanity. It was an animal, worse, because animals you could interact with, communicate with. This thing only consumed, pissed, and shit itself, made noise, and slept.

Sometimes Missy had dreams where she remembered what she thought it would be like if she ever had children. Dressing them up, reading them bedtime stories, snuggling in bed together while watching favorite movies. She shoved them out of her consciousness as soon as she woke. Otherwise, she might never get out of bed again.

They got by thanks to government aid, disability checks

and the sanity offered by the daily escape to her job as a retail manager. The state paid for a caretaker to come five days a week so she could make a living, pretend to live a life of normalcy. This week, it wasn't going well. The caretaker had called in sick. She wasn't coming. It was a Wednesday.

Missy informed her own work of her absence and began going through the motions of a weekend day. Changing the forty-five-pound child's diaper while it flailed in rebellion. Hooking up a bag of nutrients to the child's feeding tube. Trying to spoon feed it some yogurt. Washing its face and hands after, and wrestling clean clothes onto it. Getting through the day, repeating it all two more times. Trying to get the thing to fall asleep.

That night it wouldn't sleep and just kept moaning. A baby monitor that the social worker had helped her set up kept her abreast of every horrible noise. She turned it off around midnight. The noises were loud enough to keep her awake still. The apartment was tiny, one bedroom, one bathroom. It's crib was set up in the living room where a couch would have gone. Social services had gotten her into this place, close by the hospital for the many, inevitable coming emergencies.

The noises it made were semi-constant. It couldn't hear itself, and of all things, the vocal cords worked fine. This child was a non-stop cacophony of a jazz band tuning. Light moaning was a daily occurrence for various reasons, and Missy could only do her best to go through the checklist of resolutions. Check the diaper, offer it food, help it get unstuck. All options were exhausted, yet it continued to yell.

On occasion, rare occasion, the thing would reach for her, try to pull itself onto her lap or in her arms. Missy's heart would stop in those moments and her thoughts would grow dark. It was the only time she questioned *"why her, why them?"* She couldn't stand to return the affection for long without breaking down, so tried to avoid touching it as much as possible. The wailing grew louder.

After a few more hours she got up, wrestled the child into a massive stroller, wrapped a thick blanket around her and headed yet again to the hospital she loathed so well.

Several hours later, they went home the same way, a prescription for liquid antibiotics tucked in her backpack. A urinary tract infection, they'd said. Social services would be following up in a couple of days, they also said. Missy wanted to tell them they always did.

The moaning should have gotten better with the medication, but it got worse. The care worker called in sick again. At least at work, Missy could have snuck a nap in the storeroom at work. Not here. Not when the child never seemed to sleep, and the moaning filled every crack and crevice of the apartment.

Missy tried putting the child on the floor. Often the sensations and textures it found while flailing around were enough to distract it for a while. It just laid there, flopping limbs around from time to time. Missy watched as a tear escaped from its forever shut eyes and for a moment, a knife ripped through her soul. She pushed the feeling out as fast as it had come. There was no point in loving something that could never love her back. Getting attached just meant hurting more when it did die.

Staring at its face helped push away any attachment that would fester. Its face was a feminine, distorted copy of her ex. The one she'd lived with for two years before that day, before that visit to the emergency department. He who had talked about marriage someday, who made pizzas with her and worked with her to build whole worlds in their favorite video games.

It had his sandy blonde hair that Missy kept shaved on the

child to prevent it from being a hazard. The thing also had his square jaw that should have ended in a squared chin, but instead kind of melted into the neck. The nose began normal enough, a hint of his Nordic ski-jump, but after the hump widened and grew flat. She imagined it's eyes, if it had developed any, would have been the same color as her ex's. Instead, it had wide-set bulges that never opened. Lashes and crud grew around the edges. It could cry, when upset or in pain.

The doctors didn't like to give it pain meds. They said pain medication would increase the likelihood of accidental death. Would that be so bad, Missy wondered, a painless, controlled death?

Friday the caregiver texted the word "sorry," and Missy, numb inside, let her own work know she wouldn't be in another day. "You're out of PTO." Her boss had texted back. "FMLA" was the only response Missy gave. She didn't even know if she still qualified for any more FMLA time. Luckily, bringing up anything related to not meeting the law or discriminating against someone with a disabled child to the giant retail corporation, got them off her back.

Saturday the moaning hadn't ceased, regardless of the regular administration of the antibiotics. They bundled up and went back to the emergency department early in the morning. It was the quietest time to go, Missy knew. They couldn't find anything wrong this time. She felt delirious with lack of sleep and cried when they told her there was nothing else they could do. She sat in the room crying for half an hour after discharge before she could find it in her to take the moaning bag of deformed child home.

They passed some woods on the return walk. A green belt connected their street to a park, cutting through the city. It looked so peaceful there. As they passed the entrance, the child calmed to cooing and reached one deformed, skinny arm towards the trees. Missy frowned and hurried home. That night was another sleepless night of moans. She briefly considered slitting her own wrists.

That morning, as the sun rose, an idea came to her. Maybe, somehow, there was something about the woods which calmed the thing. Missy left the house wearing the sweats she had slept in, that she had been wearing for two days. They walked to the woods and pushed in.

The child stilled, visibly comforted. The moans turned to coos again. Her breathing became more regular. Missy walked through the greenbelt, leaving the trail, and turning deeper into the forest. The further she went, the calmer the child became. They continued on for a couple of hours. Missy had no idea the woods were this deep. When they reached a dead end, a small clearing surrounded by trees and boulders, the child had fallen asleep.

Missy sat on the ground. Her bones hurt. Her head ached. All her thoughts were fuzzy. Seeing the child so serene bent her so hard inside that the world tilted. No, she'd just tipped over from exhaustion. A single thought pinged through her mind, a whisper at first that became louder with each trip around. "*Leave her,*" said the thought, "*she's happy here. Leave her and go home and sleep.*"

The thought continued until it was the only sound in Missy's brain. Like a chorus chanting at her to jump in the water, it repeated, relentless. In a trance, Missy got up and began walking home. A sense of serenity descended upon her as she strolled. A peace she wasn't sure if she'd ever known before. The walk back was a surreal dream. Entering the dark apartment slapped her back into reality.

"Oh God!" Missy said, panicked, "Oh God, oh God, oh God." She turned and took a step back when another thought hit her, and she pulled out her phone to dial for help.

"911, where is your emergency?"

"Someone, someone's taken my baby?" The words came out scratchy, unsure.

"Okay, ma'am, I need you to tell me where you are, and we'll get you help immediately."

Missy rattled off her address and continued to talk to the dispatcher while waiting. The words pouring from her mouth surprised her. She didn't know where they came from. They'd been about to go for a walk, she'd said, when she realized she forgot something in the apartment, so she ran back inside. When she came out, the stroller was gone. "Please, find my baby," she begged. *Who am I?* She thought.

The police came and Missy repeated the same story, adding on that they were going for a walk because her daughter, Emily, hadn't been feeling well. More police came. Strangers volunteered to help. Hours passed. Night came. The officers suggested she try to get some sleep. Like a zombie, she walked to her bedroom, leaving several other people convened in her kitchen. She hit the bed and passed out. In the night, someone began shaking her awake. It was Nora, the caretaker, who had been sick. *She looks fine now*, Missy thought.

"Missy," Nora told her. "They found Emily."

Missy allowed herself to be led by the hand, back into her kitchen, where a grim-faced officer waited next to a woman in a suit. A blanket had been found in the woods nearby, they told her. This allowed them to use dogs to track the scent. The stroller had been found. Emily was dead. Coyotes had found her before they could.

"Coyotes?" Missy said, bewildered, "like in the cartoons?"

"She's in shock," came Nora's voice from behind her. "Oh my god Missy, I'm so sorry." Nora began crying. The sound felt unreal to Missy, rehearsed and theatrical, like she'd heard in a movie once.

Missy felt tears run down her cheeks and she questioned how that was possible when she still felt so numb inside.

The officer and the lady in the suit left information with Nora, who thanked them. Nora led Missy back to bed and tucked her in. They both knew there was no one to call for help or give the news to. Missy slept without interruption for the first time in over six years.

When she awoke, almost 48 hours had passed. She got up, stripped down, and took a shower. A feeling snuck in, the sense someone was watching. She yanked back the shower curtain, expecting Nora, and found an empty bathroom. The door to the hall was open. Did I leave the door open, she wondered. "Nora?" Missy called out, leaning forward out of the bathtub. No one answered. She got out and dried off.

Her body shook with hunger and she went to the kitchen to make something. Biting into a piece of toast, a wave of nausea almost dropped her to the floor. A new single-sentence thought pervaded her brain on repeat. *What did I do?* She couldn't answer, wouldn't dare answer. The thought became a thumping, rhythmic disco note behind everything she did. *What did I do? What did I do?*

Despite the horrible combination of hunger and nausea, Missy felt lighter than she ever had. Some part of her wanted to sing, to dance. It was over. The punishment, the torture, it was finally over. She was a monster, a fucking ruthless evil monster, and now she could sleep, she could finally sleep. Or she could leave! What if she made friends and did things after work? She might even meet someone and have sex again! The jubilance made her maniacal. *This is what it feels like to be evil.*

Nora came by that day. It was easy for Missy to slip back

into her numbness while they planned.

"A cremation would be best," Nora told her. "Keep Emily in your memory the way she was."

An unhinged giggle escaped from Missy. The horror on Nora's face flashed sanity into Missy and she began blubbering about a time Emily made her laugh, being silly. She tried to make herself cry.

It worked, though, and once it started, it came out in torrents. A category five hurricane of pain and suffering whirl-winded through her body. She didn't know this much emotion could exist, did exist inside her. Nora came around and held her. The two women rocked back and forth while Missy screamed in an emotional agony and release, she'd never known before.

A few days later, Missy went to pick up the cremains. She felt amazing. The feeling of being watched had continued here and there, but she knew it was just her getting used to being alone. Not having to constantly be in the presence of another living thing was a little jarring, that's all.

"Hi Emily," she'd said to the container once they were both in the car. At home Missy placed the box on her dresser. The living room had been cleared of the toddler bed with railings and all the medical equipment the government had rented for them. No sign of the child remained where a visitor could see it.

That night, Missy went out dancing. She was only twenty-seven, she still had time.

A taxi dropped her off at home, alone, after the bars closed. Inside, still drunk, she ate two pieces of cheap white sandwich bread with nothing on them, chugged a glass of water, and stumbled into her bedroom. The dreamless sleep of the intoxicated welcomed her. The booze wore off and she slipped into the REM stage, and then all the sudden, a sound.

The sound of pained moaning.

Missy jerked awake and scanned her bedroom. Nothing was out of place. The box containing the cremains sat on her dresser, glowing in the moonlight from the open window.

The moaning came again, not from the box. Missy got up and wandered a few steps from the bed, pulling off the tight, flashy clothes she'd worn dancing. The moaning had stopped, and she wondered if it had been her brain playing a trick on her. She listened to that moaning for the last several years and wasn't sure for how many more years her brain would keep playing it. A song from the radio of her life, looping. There were some semi-clean sweatpants and a tee shirt draped over a plastic chair. She smelled them and put them on.

In the kitchen, she found the water glass from earlier and poured another, slurping it down with relish. The front door latch was unlocked. Staring it at while she drank, she couldn't remember if she'd locked it behind her. She had forgotten to lock it before, a silent, unconscious wish for someone to come in and end things.

She realized she didn't want something to happen to her anymore. The deadbolt thunked into placed with a satisfactory noise. A soft moaning permeated the night. Missy froze, ear tilted upwards to find the source of the sound.

Not from the neighbors above, or on either side. The bedroom? The bedroom. It was coming from the bedroom. Missy crept back, water glass in hand. She pushed the door open and flipped on the light. Nothing appeared as the obvious source.

She turned on the bedside lamp before crossing back and turning off the bedroom light. The bed was too inviting, and she was still a little buzzed. Her head hit the pillow and sunk into the fabric in bliss. Sleep washed over her again in gentle waves. The moaning cut through and made her eyes snap open. She sat up and searched for the source across the dim room.

Again, the noise sounded as though it came from the other room. Missy jumped up and marched out into the kitchen. The moaning stopped, then resumed, but now, coming from her bedroom. She shuffled back towards the room. The door had swung half shut when she left. Her hands pushed forward, and the hollow door swung inwards to reveal the contents.

Nothing had changed in the seconds since she left. The moaning again. Missy took a step towards the box of cremains. The sound became louder.

"Emily?" she asked into the empty room. The noise stopped.

She took another step towards the box. "Emily?" she asked again.

A soft scuffling noise behind her. Missy whirled in place to confront the sound and came face to face with the floating body of her child, shredded by coyotes. Her belly was torn out, internal organs dangling and mangled. Sections of muscle on the arms and thighs were ripped down to the bone, torn into threads. The face was still perfectly deformed, somehow untouched by the wild dogs.

Emily's face lifted up towards her. Her mouth opened. She whispered, "mama."

The child wrapped its arms around Missy's neck, snuggling her close. "Mama, you can hear me now."

Missy screamed.

The Bee Witch

Kyle strolled through the backyard on the beautiful August day, envisioning the changes he'd make to accommodate his new son, due at any moment. There was an old wooden fort in the yard, built by the previous owners. It needed a fresh coat of paint, and the rope swing replaced, but it would hold up. Not that the kid would play on it for a few years, but it didn't cost anything to dream about. A fat, fuzzy bumble bee flew past him and landed on the hydrangeas to collect pollen. He stopped to lean down and pull some weeds from the flower garden lining the driveway.

A lilting, feminine voice cleared her throat. "Hello. What a lovely garden you have."

He hadn't heard anyone walk up the gravel drive. Normally it crunched loudly when anyone walked on it, even the neighbor's small dog. He looked up and assessed his visitor. "Hello."

She resembled a character from a children's book, or someone cosplaying at the renaissance fair. A long golden yellow skirt hid her shoes. The skirt was covered in black lacy embroidery that showcased a hexagon-shaped pattern. A long, baggy knit cardigan sweater in a slightly lighter color of golden yellow hung open to reveal a thin black hoody underneath. She had the hood up.

"I'm Mel." She curtsied. "I love your flowers. It looks like you really care about bees.

"Thanks, uh, this was all here when we moved in, but we're trying to do a good job of maintaining it. We're new to the neighborhood."

Her face delighted at his answer. "How good of you! Do you know what kind of grass you have?"

"Oh, uh, I think it's a mix of Kentucky bluegrass and fine fescue species?"

"That's wonderful for bees! They love that kind of grass."

"Yeah, I've heard." Kyle stood, finished with his weeding, and wiped his hands on his jeans. He took a backward step towards the house.

She took a step, too, following him onto the lawn. "I'm raising money for the Bee Foundation. We're selling honey and artisan crafts made from beeswax. The money goes towards protecting the local wild bee population."

She presented a bag that he hadn't noticed before. Also yellow, it was patterned with smiling black bumblebees. From inside she produced a small jar of honey and held it up in the sunlight. She stared into the glowing amber jar, grinning. Her eyes became lost in the liquid, and her chest heaved.

"Oh, I see." Kyle smiled and took another step back. Their

inner-city neighborhood attracted an eclectic sort. Although, it was more common to see a nuclear family with a stroller than it was to see one of the local oddballs. "Well, my wife is pregnant, so she can't have any honey right now. I appreciate the offer, though."

"Honey is wonderful for pregnant women! It's full of vitamins. Guarantees a healthy baby!"

"Well, the doctor told us no honey, so...doctor's orders. Sorry."

Mel wrinkled her nose and looked from side to side before refocusing on her mark. "Okay." She rummaged around in her bag and produced a short, fat candle wrapped in fabric. "A beeswax candle, then! It'll smell wonderful in your house. Help your wife to relax."

"We don't burn candles. Thanks though."

They stood, silent, staring each other down. Mel continued holding the candle out to him from the edge of the lawn.

Kyle cleared his throat. "Well, I better get back to the wife." He turned and began walking towards the house.

"It's for a good cause!" She called out behind him.

"Sorry!" He sang out the word without turning around.

"You'll regret it, if you don't!"

Kyle stopped walking. "Excuse me?" He half turned and regarded her over his shoulder.

The woman took another step towards him. "The bee populations have been diminishing. They're dying. If we don't take steps to protect them. We need them for every vegetable we grow. Every flower we smell. If the bees go, we won't be long after."

He turned to face her. "I said, no thank you." He wasn't an angry man, but he knew being six foot, four inches, and solidly built, he could intimidate when he wanted. He stood, arms akimbo, feet turned out, legs strong and stiff, punctuating the stance with a glare. Holding the expression started to give him a headache.

"You don't even know how much they are. Don't you ever do anything nice to help someone else?"

"I'm going to have to ask you to leave." He folded his arms across his chest and lifted his chin. A bead of sweat tickled his hairline.

Mel stared back at him, unmoving. She reminded him of a render; unnaturally still.

Kyle turned and stormed into the house, shutting the door firmly behind him.

Inside, Saoirse hung up the phone and rubbed her expansive belly with love. Everything was coming together. After many failed attempts, they were finally pregnant with a desperately wanted little baby. Their due date was nigh. They'd finally found the perfect house to raise children in, to grow old in. It had seemed impossible to find a house to buy within their budget, new listings sold before they could even tour. Yet this house had appeared right on cue, and they were smart enough to make an immediate offer. It was a new neighborhood to them, but it already felt familiar. Now if only she could get the darned internet working.

Kyle wandered into the room, shaking his head. "I just had the weirdest conversation."

"Oh?" Saoirse stood on her toes to kiss his cheek. "What happened?"

"There's some kind of crazy woman outside, trying to get me to buy bee stuff or something."

Saoirse raised an eyebrow. "Bee stuff?"

"Yeah, go look. She won't leave the yard."

She waddled to the window and lifted the curtain to peek outside. "There's no one there now?"

Kyle came up behind her and pulled the curtain further

back. There was no sign that the strange woman had ever been there.

Saoirse wrapped one arm around her husband and squeezed. "Would it make you feel any better to know that the internet guy is coming tomorrow?"

"Yes, it does." Kyle hugged her back tightly. "I don't know how we were supposed to survive parental leave without Wi-Fi."

"We still have our phones." Saoirse shrugged, ever good-natured.

"NOT THE SAME!' Kyle roared in a joking voice and mimed throwing a chair across the room.

"Alright, alright, calm down BamBam. He'll be here between eight and ten a.m."

Kyle grunted and leaned over, pretending to gorilla-walk out of the room.

Saoirse basked in the afternoon sunlight that streamed through the windows and went through her birthing checklist one more time in her head. A noise distracted her. A small bee flew in a lazy zigzag across the room. "Where did you come from little guy?" She grabbed an empty glass and an ad that had come in the mail, trapped the bee, and carefully walked it outside. The bee was freed next to a large rhododendron, and she imagined it buzzing a "thank you" as it flew off.

The next morning Kyle had already left for work by the time the internet guy finally arrived. After climbing all over their house, he announced he'd have to run a new ethernet cable to get the whole house on the same network.

"It's an easy fix," he told Saoirse. "I just have to drill a couple small holes to run the cable through. Where's a good place down here?" She motioned to the wall behind the couch, where a dime-sized hole wouldn't be noticed. "Will the router still work behind there?"

"Shouldn't be a problem by the time I'm done." He flashed her a goofy smile. "Congrats, by the way. What are you having?"

"Thank you, it's a boy." Saoirse beamed and sipped her tea.

"Nice." The man pulled the couch away from the wall and kneeled down with his drill.

That night, Saoirse had to drag Kyle away from flicking through their streaming services, now in full color on their brand new, ridiculously large television. "I want to go for a walk," she tugged on his hand. "It's good for the baby and will help my labor."

The golden hour made the neighborhood feel ethereal, and the happy couple strolled arm in arm. They made it to the end of the block and stopped to consider which direction to go. A tiny bee appeared and flitted about their heads. Kyle waived it off. Saoirse leaned closer to him and attempted to cover her large belly with her spread hands. "It looks like the one that was in our house yesterday."

"Oh?" Kyle tried to waive it off again. "Must be a hive, or a nest, somewhere nearby. Did I ever tell you I'm allergic to bees?" The bee finally departed off to their left, and in silent agreement, they turned right. A few houses had neighbors out in their yards, tending to flowers and shrubbery. They waived to anyone they saw.

"I don't remember." Saoirse struggled to keep pace with him. "Are you worried? Should we head home?"

"Nah, I'm sure it'll be fine. I just worry little Rollie's gonna be allergic too."

Another bee appeared. They sped up. Saoirse pulled on Kyle's hand to keep him from leaving her behind. "We'll get him checked right away. We can get an EpiPen or something if we need to."

Kyle nodded and kept up his pace.

After twenty more feet, a second bee joined the first, and the two danced a ballet around the strolling couple. Making eye contact, Saoirse and Kyle turned to start walking back. "I'm not allergic," Saoirse offered, "but I don't want any problems either. We're so close."

Kyle reached over and rubbed her shoulders, "Can't be too careful."

A third bee merged into the parade. They were close to jogging by the time they made it back to their front door. Kyle jogged up the front porch and fumbled the keys several times before turning the lock. Saoirse awkwardly hopped from side to side after him, unable to run properly, and dashed inside. Now safely in the house, they burst into laughter. Did they really just run from bees?

"Ooh!" Saoirse startled, grabbing her belly. "I think Rollie just kicked me!"

Later that night, Saoirse realized the kicking was happening every twenty minutes for the same duration each time. She sat up abruptly. "Kyle, I think he's coming! It's happening."

"Oh shit!" Kyle jumped up and ran for their overnight bags before dashing outside. At the car, he opened the back door to set the bags inside, when a lone bee flew out. He watched it pass by and head towards the house, where Saoirse was waddling down to him. They looked at each other and shrugged. During the drive he tells her, "I don't get it. All the windows were rolled up." Saoirse was busy trying to keep track of her breathing.

The labor was easy and uneventful, but thoroughly exhausting, even though it goes quickly for a first baby. They stay only one night in the hospital before the family is discharged to go home.

When they arrive back at the house, Kyle runs for the door to clear the way for Saoirse to get inside. When the door cracks, the buzzing noise hits him as though a lawnmower was running in the background. At first, he thought he'd left the TV or another appliance on and pushed open the door to see. Inside, a hoard of bees flies in wild loops and zigzags. They can't find their way out. He stopped, hand stuck to the doorknob, watching the movement inside his house.

"Everything okay?" Saoirse called from behind him, pulling herself out of the car.

"Don't come in! There's bees in the house."

"What? How?"

"I don't know, just get back in the car and shut the door."

Saoirse lowered herself back onto her pillow in the passenger seat. The car is warming already, and Kyle took the keys with him. Closing the door meant they might quickly be sweltering without air conditioning. Rollie snores softly from behind her. A bee flew by. Saoirse pulled her legs in and shut the door.

Inspiration struck Kyle and he runs around to the back entrance of the house. Unlocking the back door, he pulls out a large box fan from the storage closet. He sets it in the doorway so that it will suck air from the house out to the backyard and turns it on, then runs back around to the front. He stops at the car briefly to make sure Saoirse and Rollie are safe. She stares up at him and throws her hands up in question. "I've got it," he yells through the window, "just a few more minutes."

Back at the front door, he opens it wide and dives for the broom they keep near the entryway. Making giant sweeping motions through the air, he drives the bees towards the open back door of the house. The buzzing of the bees soon disappears, and only the droning of the box fan remains. He does one last sweep of the house before shutting the doors and going to help his family inside.

When everyone is settled in the house, Saoirse listens to his story, eyebrows knitted in disbelief. "I know!" Kyle tells her, "It's crazy. I'm going to call an exterminator this week and have them check out the house."

"If you think we need to? I always thought bees were good. That we needed more of them. Isn't there some other way to take care of this?"

"Maybe. I'll ask them, maybe there's some kind of humane thing to do. We just got to get rid of them."

Saoirse reached down to rub her belly and found it missing. She glances down in confusion before her eyes find her sleeping baby, still tucked into his carrier. "I heard once that you can call some beekeepers, and they have a way to come get the bees. Take them back to their hives."

"I'll ask. I don't know if they'll come out for just a few bees, but there's got to be something they can do."

Saoirse frowned, she'd been a vegetarian for years and hates the idea of harm coming to any creature. "How did they even get in?" She asks and unbuckles the baby from his seat before settling down on the couch. Rollie stirs in her arms and remains snoring.

"Good question." Kyle begins to inspect the house.

A moment later, buzzing alerts Saoirse and she turns to see a small, fuzzy bee crawl over the back of the couch. "Kyle! Bee!" She scoots away, holding her baby tight to her chest.

Kyle rushes across the room and slaps it with a magazine. A mess of black, green, and yellow goo with legs sticking out is embedded into their fabric sofa. He crawls onto the couch next to her and looks at the wall behind them. "Saoirse, was there always a hole in this wall?"

"Huh? Oh! The internet guy did that!"

"I think we found where our bees are coming from."

"Oh no! What? No. I didn't realize!"

Kyle goes to get the duct tape.

The rest of the night passed quietly, except for nursings and diapers every two to four hours. By the morning, it seemed the bee problem was over, and the exhausted parents had forgotten their plan. It's easy to forget important things when you're that sleep deprived.

On the second day home, Kyle searched for his keys and wallet to go get groceries. After a fruitless forty-five minutes, he found them both sitting in the refrigerator. He asks Saoirse if she put them there. "No?" She asks, just as confused. "Why would I do that?"

Shaking his head, Kyle pockets his items and heads for the door. He returns a few minutes later to find his shoes.

Saoirse fell asleep on the couch while watching Rollie sleep in his bassinet. The lazy afternoon passed. An hour goes by, and a noise wakes her. Buzzing, she realizes, eyes popping open wide. Another bee.

The bee flies around her face and lands on her cheek. She freezes, watching it from her peripheral vision. It walks across her face to the edge of her nostril, probing it. The bee begins to creep inside. She exhales hard, and the bee takes flight, disturbed. The buzzing continues close by. She sits up, eyes traveling over the edge of the bassinet to Rollie. Bees swarm the inside of the crib. Rollie is still, and wide awake, watching them fly around his head. His little body is covered in them, exploring his belly, arms, and legs. At least a dozen bees fill the crib.

Holding her breath, Saoirse tries to shoo them away. Some leave, but immediately return. Remembering Kyle's trick, she runs for the box fan. Bees dance around her at random through the house. She dodges and pirouettes, finds the fan and spins to reverse course. Back at the crib, she turns on the lowest setting, aiming it inside the bassinet. It works. The bees lift off in annoyance and fly around the room, looking for something else to explore. When almost no bees are left, she reaches in and lifts her son out with the precision of a brain surgeon.

She snatches her phone off the coffee table and sprints for the front door. The bees have multiplied. The front door crawls with them, a moving kaleidoscope of yellow and black. A bee lands on her forearm and stings. She yelps, almost drops the baby, then turns and runs for the stairs. Rollie begins to wail, disturbed by his mother's alarm.

Another needle prick to the back of her calf. She stumbles and drops onto one knee with a crack on the hard wood stairs. She gets up and starts again. More stinging, now to her back and hips. Bursting into the upstairs hall, she sees the nearest room, sprints to it, and slams the door behind her. Just inside the door, she gasps, struggling to catch her breath. A sharp pain in her side accompanies the burning stings. She can hear them, buzzing outside the door. Louder all of a sudden from below, and she looks down.

One little bee crawls underneath the door into the room. Saoirse sets Rollie on the bed and slams a book down on top of the bee before it can take flight. They're in the guest room, and their extra storage place. A large box in the corner is filled with present wrapping supplies. Inside she finds a roll of packing tape and begins to seal the door shut. The bees are creeping in and taking flight. She alternates between slapping them with a book and taping the door shut. At last, the cracks are sealed, and she runs around like mad, smashing the remaining intruders before they can get to her son. Rollie cries, insistent and loud.

Saoirse gathers him up in her arms and begins to nurse him, trying to calm both of them in the process. With her free hand, she pulls out her phone to call Kyle and yells as soon as he picks up. "There's bees everywhere! Come home!"

"What, still? Okay, I'm in the checkout line. I'll be there soon."

"Kyle! They're everywhere! Get home now!"

A bee flies into her mouth and stings the back of her throat. She screams and drops the phone. Bees swarm in from the heating vent. They cover her. She hears Kyle calling her name from the phone on the floor. Her body burns from the previous stings and her mouth fills with bees as she tries to scream again. The screaming becomes choking and gargling as her throat is coated in the crawling insects. Rollie continues to nurse, blissfully unaware. All at once, the bees began to sting. She falls backwards on the bed as they invade her, crawling deep inside. Her last act of living is to let Rollie fall gently next to her on the bed. He remains unstung, but cries, frustrated that the nipple has pulled free from his mouth.

Time passes.

The front door flies open and slams against the wall. Kyle rushes into the house and finds it empty downstairs. There is no noise except from the TV that Saoirse had fallen asleep to earlier. He darts up the stairs, which comes alive with the swarm as he enters. The bees flock to his body, coating him as he swings madly through the air to ward them off. He makes it up the steps in seconds and pounds on the closed door. "Saoirse!" He screams, "Rollie!" His throat begins to close as the stings pile on. Kyle claws at his neck; final breath already taken. He falls to his knees, beating on the door with the last of his failing strength.

The bees meander about, bored, looking for nectar, and finding nothing of interest. Soon after, a strange woman enters the house. She wears a long black skirt with fat, happy bumble bees embroidered around it. This matches her yellow cardigan, which has tiny enamel bees for the buttons, and a black scarf, pinned at the shoulder with a large honeycomb shaped brooch. The bees come to her and gently caress her hair and skin, welcoming her before resuming their search of the house.

She climbs the stairs as though gliding against gravity, head held high. At the top, she reaches over Kyle's swollen, lumpy body, and pushes the door open, breaking Saoirse's seal. The woman wrinkles her nose in disgust at the site of the many bees caught in the packing tape. Some remain alive, wiggling. So many fallen soldiers, and so many squished bodies covering the floor.

On the bed, the surviving bees lift from Saoirse's body, leaving her slightly less swollen, but still dead. She is frozen, suffocated by the many suicide fighters. The strange woman stands over Saoirse, watching, pleased. "Why hello little man," she speaks to the gurgling baby, unharmed by the bees which explore his soft skin. "What a fine little prince you'll make."

He began to mew his soft infant cry again as the woman picks him up, "ssshhhhh," she says, comforting him against her shoulder. "Let's go get you some honey."

It's A Girl

The mail guy was late. They had to get to Bobby's last prenatal appointment already. Ben rapped his knuckles on the door. There'd been too many thefts in the area to leave a giant box on the porch. The truck turned into their short driveway. Ben opened the front door to collect the box and felt the heat of the Texas summer sun slap him across the face. The driver fished around in the back of his truck for a few seconds before pulling out the large box containing a car seat and walking it up the steps. "Here you go," the driver handed off the package, "So what are you having?"

Ben flashed a quick, annoyed smile. "Thanks, having a girl."

"Oh!" The driver shook his head "no" as he returned to his truck. "I'd be jealous if it were a boy, but a girl? No thanks."

Ben walked it into the house, meeting Bobby in the living room. "Oh good," she said, taking a labored breath, "let's go."

He helped her to the car before getting in the driver's seat. Only a minute passed before pulled onto the main road. It was a short drive to the hospital, one of the biggest reasons they'd chosen to rent here. Bobby stretched and adjusted the seatbelt, "Can we go over the birth plan again, please?"

He reached over and squeezed her knee, "I know it; we're fine. Everything will be fine."

"Nope, nuh-uh. Black women die in childbirth twice as often as white women in this state. Probably more now that all the doctors are leaving. I have no reassurance it's going to be fine."

Ben looked out the window and sighed. "Okay."

She threaded her fingers through his and lifted his hand to kiss the back of it. "I know you think I'm just angry for no reason sometimes, but please listen to me here?"

Ben flashed her a smile, "I am, babe, I am."

At the hospital, they waited for over an hour after their appointment was supposed to begin before the doctor saw them. Both played on their phones to pass the time, Ben in the chair, Bobby on the bed with her feet up in the straps, and the cold breeze from the air conditioning chilling her thighs. The exam table faced the door, so she had pulled the privacy screen before lying down.

They heard the door open, both looked up, and the screen was ripped back, exposing Bobby's uncovered genitals to the hallway. A large, older, white man stood at the open door. "Hello! Who do we have here?" His voice boomed across the tiny room.

Bobby shrieked. "Can you please shut the door?"

"Oh!" The man stumbled in and looked around confused,

before shutting the door behind him. "Sorry 'bout that." He came into the room and offered his hand to Ben. "I'm Doctor Reeves. It's nice to meet you."

Ben stood up to shake the Doctor's hand. "I'm Ben, and this is Bobby," he gestured behind the doctor.

Dr. Reeves slowly spun in a circle, an egg rocking in place, until he faced her, "Well, hello Bobby!" He rubbed her on the knee. "Didn't mean to startle you there."

"It's fine. Where's Doctor Mullins?"

"She's held up in surgery. Normally, I'd cover for her there, but now I'm covering for her here." He punctuated the statement with braying laughter.

He leaned over her, getting close to her face. She could smell his lunch. "You're here for your forty-week check-up?" He asked.

"Yeah," She tried to retract her face into the pillow.

"Well, suppose I'd better take a look and see how you're doing!" He smiled after everything he said. The smiling was not reassuring her.

He took a seat on the stool in front of the bed and started to pull on a glove from the bedside dispenser. She pulled her knees shut. "Don't you want to wash your hands before you do that?"

"Oh! Oh." Dr. Reeves' face turned red, and he grimaced, before getting up to wash his hands in the sink. Bobby looked down at Ben, who was busy reading on his phone. The doctor returned to the stool and pulled gloves on to begin the inspection.

"So, what are you having?"

Bobby tried to see the doctor's face as she answered, but he was staring intently into her vulva as he probed at her cervix.

"A girl."

He pulled his fingers out. "Can't feel any dilation of the

cervix yet. I'm going to check how things look. You're due Monday?"

"Yes." She felt the cold discomfort of the speculum being inserted. The clicks made her tense as it forcibly stretched her open.

"And what are we going to name the little angel?"

"Ashley."

"Ashanti? Like the singer?"

"Ashley. Ow!"

"Sorry about that." He ripped the speculum out, making Bobby wince and yelp again.

Dr. Reeves turned to Ben, "Are you the father?"

Confusion flitted across Ben's features. "I'm her husband, yes."

"Congratulations, everything looks fine. She could go into labor any day now, so make sure you're aware of the signs. Sometimes women can get anxious and confused around this time, and we don't want to waste a bunch of time when she's not ready yet."

Ben tilted his head back and forth, rolling the responses around. "Thanks doctor, I'll be sure to read up on that."

"You're very welcome, son. Take care now." Dr. Reeves stood and wiggled Bobby's toes on her nearest foot. "Take care of that baby now! Ya hear?"

Bobby blinked hard and stared at the Doctor, who was clearly waiting for her response.

"Sure will."

"Good girl." He tapped her on the foot one last time and turned to leave.

On the ride home Bobby turned on the air conditioning full blast. "What a fucking creep."

Ben turned down the air. "What do you mean?"

"Well, wouldn't wash his hands, for one."

"He's a doctor, Bobby. I'm sure he knows what he's doing."

"Fifty percent more likely to die in childbirth, Ben."

"Alright," he sighed. "Alright."

Her contractions started a few days later. Ben didn't believe her until he felt her belly quiver under his hand and timed them himself. She took a lukewarm bath while he packed the car. At the hospital they were welcomed with kindness and checked into a birthing suite without issue. They were discussing the merits of an epidural when the door flew open. Dr. Reeves stood there, dressed in undersized scrubs and his usual smile. "Well, isn't it the happy couple!" Bobby's heart dropped.

An hour later, they were wheeling her into surgery, "I don't want a c-section," She grasped Ben's hand tightly in her own. "I want Dr. Mullins."

"Shhh." Ben leaned over and kissed her on the forehead. "I'll be right there. Dr. Reeves said your blood pressure is skyrocketing. We need to get Ashley out now."

Thirty minutes later, Ben was holding a mewling baby. Nearby, Bobby strained to see through the plastic window separating her view from her opened belly. She watched Dr. Reeves approach her husband, speaking in a hushed tone. "I can't stop the bleeding. I'll need to put her under. You'll have to wait outside."

A mask was placed over her face. The room went black.

In the birthing suite, Ben waited. Pacing, he cradled the newly cleaned infant who now slept on his bare chest. Dr. Reeves came into the room a couple of hours after Ben had left the OR. He wasn't smiling and motioned for Ben to sit down.

"I'm sorry," he began. Ben's eyes welled up as the doctor began talking. "She won't be able to have any more children."

"What?" The growing tightness in Ben's chest stalled. "What did you say?"

"I had to remove part of her uterus to get the bleeding to stop. I did everything I could. I'm so sorry."

"She's alright?"

"She'll be fine after she recovers. I'll file the paperwork today, gotta make sure she's placed on the registry of non-menstruating biological women within forty-eight hours of this kind of procedure. I wouldn't want this to cause any problems for you later when she's not providing you with more children."

"She's fine." Bobby's shoulders relaxed and Ashley stirred in his arms. "When can I see her?"

"They're bringing her back right now. Again, I'm really sorry son. I know being a father is such a joy in life. If needed, you might be able to get a surrogate, adopt, or try with someone else."

"What?"

They were interrupted by Bobby being wheeled into the room. "Ben!" She coughed his name into existence. She had two black eyes and looked like she'd lost fifty pounds. "Ashley."

Ben placed the baby into her arms and looked up at the sound of Dr. Reeves leaving the room.

~ ~ ~

At the one-month check-up, Dr. Mullins apologized for not having been there. They reassured her they were just glad everyone was fine. "We have a new test," Dr. Mullins explained after taking Ashley's weight and height. "State law requires us to administer it within the first ninety days after birth."

"Okay," Bobby jiggled Ashley gently as she started crying. "What kind of test? Do you mind?" she asked, pointing at her chest.

"Not at all. This is a family practice. You might already know that when women are born, they are born with all the eggs they will carry for the rest of their life."

"Okay," Bobby nestled her infant onto her breast. "I don't understand where this is going."

"Well, I don't exactly agree with it, but state law now requires an inspection and ultrasound be done within the first three months after birth and annually thereafter on a born female's genitals to check for growth and abnormalities."

"You want to do a vaginal exam on my baby?"

Ben stepped forward from where he'd been leaning against the wall, playing a game on his phone. "Wait, what?"

"Not a vaginal exam." Dr. Mullins held both hands up in a stop motion. "It's just visual on the outside, and then an ultrasound over her belly and hips, not inside."

"This is not acceptable." Bobby pulled a baby blanket over Ashley, hiding her from sight.

"I agree," Dr. Mullins looked down at the floor, steadied herself, and then into Bobby's eyes. "I want you to understand, this is state law now. So, if you go to another doctor, they will also require it."

Ben stepped between his wife and the doctor. "Wait. Why are you doing this? Why are they doing this?"

Dr. Mullins took a deep breath. "It's supposed to be looking for early indicators of fertility issues, since there's been such a large drop in the birthing rate. This is…supposed…to help."

Bobby felt her face grow warm and briefly wondered if Dr. Mullins could see the flushing under her dark skin. "The state wants to know how good of a baby-maker my literal baby is going to be?"

The doctor wrung her hands. "Proponents of the law also claim this will help catch sexual violence early and more often."

Ben threw his arms out between the doctor and Bobby. "What the fuck? She's a baby, only living with her mom and dad. No one's hurting her."

"I'm sure that's true, Ben. I believe you. Unfortunately, it's state law now. But hold on a second. As long as I am your doctor, we can make this as painless as possible. Technically, I already inspected Ashley, and am happy to write down that she looks fine. I just need my ultrasound tech to come and wave the wand over her for a couple seconds and then we can be done. We don't even have to take her diaper off."

"No!" Ben slapped his hand on the counter. "You're not doing this."

"Ben," Bobby reached out and took his hand. "It's fine. Dr. Mullins is trying to help us here. We need to let her do her job."

Ben whirled to face her. The clock in the room went tick. Tick. Tick. He turned towards the door. "I'll be out in the lobby."

Dr. Mullins looked into Bobby's eyes. "I'm sorry."

"It's okay." Bobby gave her a meager smile, "I get it."

On the drive home Ben toggled between speeding and slamming on the brakes. Bobby squeezed his knee. "Hey," she squeezed again, "slow down, please?"

"We need to leave Texas. We should have left when the laws started changing. It's time."

"Ben, my whole family is here. Who would watch Ashley when we're at work?"

"Well, we need to figure out something. Maybe one of your sisters can come with us."

"They've all got their own people. Besides, what makes

you think they'll even let us leave? They'd let you leave. Not me, though. Not Ashley. You know that."

Ben sniffed and blinked tears back. "Yeah," he nodded, "I know." He turned to look out the window, then let up off the accelerator.

~ ~ ~

A few years went by. Life continued as normal. Bobby had to start completing state-required pregnancy tests every six months, at her cost, despite the notes from the hospital saying it was near impossible for her to get pregnant. She started giving her pee to her sisters for their appointments. Proving they weren't pregnant allowed them to keep working and having hobbies the state deemed unsafe for pregnant women. It allowed them to continue to purchase alcohol, and pretend they had choices.

~ ~ ~

One afternoon when she was four, Ben took Ashley to the park and settled down on a bench to watch while she ran wild. He pulled out a book and tried to multi-task while keeping an eye on her. A little boy ran up to her, took her hand, and tried to pull her after him. Ben smirked as she jerked her hand back and stomped her foot. From the distance he could barely catch her indignant "No!"

The little boy stepped into Ashley and shoved her to the ground. Ben jumped up from the bench and began marching. Ashley scrambled to her feet and planted a well-placed kick to the boy's groin. He screamed, high-pitched and startling. Ben began jogging.

Another man swooped in and yanked Ashley away from the boy by her arm. "Hey!" Ben yelled and sped up, crossing the remaining distance in seconds, and pulling her from the stranger's hands.

"Woah," yelled the man. "Is this your girl? She just

attacked my son!"

"Your son shoved my daughter, Buddy. I think you better calm right down there." Ben pulled Ashely behind him.

The little boy spoke up, "I just wanted to play with her, and she hurt me!"

"You see?" The man motioned at the kids. "He was just being nice, and she attacked him." He leaned over to try and face Ashley directly. "Good girls don't act like that. You need to apologize."

Ben pushed Ashley back behind him again, "You got it all wrong there. I watched the whole thing. He shoved her down. She did not start it."

"Is that true, Duke?" The little boy shrugged his shoulders and looked down into the dirt.

Ben turned around and picked up Ashley. He began storming back to the car as she wrapped her arms around his neck. "He hurt me first."

"I know, baby."

She kissed him on the cheek. "Thank you, Daddy."

Duke's father yelled out to their backs, "You're lucky there's no cops nearby. You know what they do with girls who don't behave now."

~ ~ ~

They got the letter a few months before Ashely's tenth birthday. Her annual fertility checks had shown her to be healthy, so she was being added to the registry of fertile women. If the family didn't inform the state of her first menstrual period, she'd be removed from their custody for negligence. Bobby cried.

Ben paced the house. If they drove non-stop, they could make it to Hobbs, New Mexico in six and a half hours.

"Just overnight bags," Bobby told him, "If they think we're

going any further than family in El Paso, we're done for."

"How do you know about this place? Are you sure they'll help us?"

"We talk," Bobby told him, "Women talk. It's hard to know if it's real, or who to trust, but if we don't try... You know she's going to have to pick a husband or be assigned one by sixteen. You know that."

Ashley came out of her room, backpack in hand. "Do I really have to ride in the trunk?"

Ben dropped to his knees and hugged her. "Baby, if they see you in the car, they'll take you away. We have to pretend you're staying at gramma's and that mom, and I are just on a trip for the weekend. It won't be comfortable, but I know you can do it."

"In New Mexico, will the teachers check my panties every week?"

"What?" Both parents spoke as one.

"My teacher said he needed to check my panties every week to see if I started my period. I don't like it, but I don't want to get in trouble."

Bobby took Ashley by the shoulders. "Does he do anything besides look?"

"No, I'd have told you if I thought he was doing anything weird."

Ben put his head in his hands. "Fuck."

"Come on, Baby, let's get you settled." Bobby took her third grader by the hand and out to the garage. They'd built her a nest in the trunk where she could lay down, cushioned on all sides by blankets and pillows. Ashley would have a phone to text her parents and keep occupied, but mostly the plan was for her to nap. Cardboard created a false bottom over her where they would lay their bags and things. Any light probing, and it would look like they were traveling with a large, wrapped present underneath their bags. Any deeper digging and they were done for.

The family pulled out of the garage as the sun rose, hoping to blend into the mess of morning traffic. Bobby reached over and took Ben's hand. He squeezed it and began heading towards the interstate. They were barely out of town when a police cruiser pulled behind them. Both parents stayed frozen, hands gripped so tight the blood left their knuckles. The cruiser's lights came on. They looked at each other.

Thank You

Thank you for having purchased The Reigns of Terror Volumes One, Two, and Three. If you enjoyed what you read, please leave a review. Reviews are the best way to communicate to publishers and other readers that you enjoyed what you read and would like to see more in this series.

I need to thank Nickel and Grace for reading every single one of these stories and even being nice enough to sometimes give constructive feedback. Thank you to Navin and Jamie for their younger person's perspective on A Good Prank, Grace hated it, so I'm glad someone liked it.

I also need to thank L & K for letting me share their story, although with some liberties taken and a different ending than what really happened with their Bee Witch. Thank you to Glenda, Sylvie and S. Z. Gray for helping me with edits and the ropes of self-publishing.

A special thanks to my dad for his feedback on A Long Drive. As a retired logger, his input on details and terminology was invaluable. Lastly, thank you especially to J & J for their editing and feedback. All of these wonderful people helped shape the final versions of the stories, and for that I am eternally grateful.

If you enjoyed this volume, please sign up for email announcements of new work on my website or follow me on social media. May your dreams be forever haunted.

-JR

https://jackreigns.com/
https://www.instagram.com/jacksterbooks/
https://www.tiktok.com/@jacksterbooks
https://bsky.app/profile/jacksterbooks.bsky.social

Printed in Great Britain
by Amazon